D0843053

THE EIGHTH DEADLY SIN

A man meets a woman at their publisher's cocktail party; he takes her out to dinner and the evening finishes in bed in his office. Afterwards, they return to their respective homes and spouses. They then embark on a casual affair which becomes more serious, at least for Mike, if not for Jane.

Then one day, she doesn't turn up to meet him — and Mike begins his quest to track her down. He knows little about Jane except what she likes in bed, and he's read her first novel from cover to cover.

The eighth deadly sin? As long as one isn't found out . . .

THE EIGHTH DEADLY SIN

Jessica Mann

·BLACK·
DAGGER
·CRIME·

First published 1976
by
Macmillan

This edition 2002 by Chivers Press
published by arrangement with
the author

ISBN 0 7540 8624 0

British Library Cataloguing in Publication Data available

Printed and bound in Great Britain by
Bookcraft, Midsomer Norton, Somerset

THE EIGHTH DEADLY SIN

PART ONE

The ungainly cereal packet, the hamster cage on the window sill, the coffee stain on the sugar; the gleam of dark glass between the orange curtains, the damp patch spreading on the oblong of white-painted hardboard which blocked off the fireplace, the wire and shreds of paper hanging from a disintegrating lampshade: if she minded them herself, Mike would be able to endure them more easily. Yet as he glanced away from Christine's dark, indifferent face, he remembered how Jane's had seemed momentarily to resemble it, and how the unexpected likeness had pleased him, because it put Jane into the class of women who presided at breakfast tables and partook of the minor squalors of family life, and reminded their children, as Christine was now reminding Samantha, to clean their teeth. Yet in this setting perhaps even Jane would grow passionless.

Christine held out the crumpled inner section of the newspaper across the table, while with her other hand she tilted the pot to pour a dribble of chilly black tea into her cup. Then she reached for a cigarette, and lustfully drew the smoke into her open mouth. She exhaled with a sigh that other pleasures rarely drew from her.

It was the same make of cigarettes that Mike had once pressed into Jane's hand, when she flinched, incredulous still at his—was it his daring which had impressed her? Or was she showing again her former inhibitions derived from the class and background which he had, to be accurate, rather suspected than observed? He could not be sure whether her dismay was at the danger or at the immorality of knocking off a packet of fags. The woman he knew had, after all, turned out very differently from his expectations.

Mike met Jane at a publisher's party. Palfrey & Blackwood were marking the occasion of publishing number ten thousand on their list of books for children and, curious juxtaposition, romantic novels. Their pious tracts of the early nineteenth century had given way to schoolgirl stories, horse books and mild science fiction. In the nineteen seventies they sold realistic descriptions of life in tower blocks and the adventures of a groupie, as well as whimsical tales of animals and elves. Mike had recently published his second volume of law cases for the young. He retold in simple language the facts of old litigation, and asked the reader to guess what the judge decided. The judgment of Solomon, the publishers told him, was reported by the teachers on their panel to have stumped everybody below the age for scripture lessons.

Christine never came with him to such events. She said that she felt like a spare dinner amongst all those creative people, but he thought that she despised, in fact, their frivolous way of making a living. She was the head of a department of radiography at a hospital in one of London's worst slums, and it was hard to argue with her conviction that she served a more useful purpose in the world than those who provided light reading matter.

Thank goodness that Samantha did not take after her mother. She was only nine years old, but inbred in her bones was the knowledge that she should deliciously defer to men. Until her husband took over the benefit of her tender tact—and Mike loathed already the unknown man who would steal his daughter from him—she remained the apple of her father's eye. Mike had a quick vision of the apple he would draw to represent Samantha: perfectly

6

rounded, yellowish green streaked with pink, a smooth, thumb-sized depression for the stalk.

Mike's drawing was confined nowadays to doodling on his papers in the office or in court. He had never been trained and thought of himself as an artist in temperament, not ability. He did not imagine that his talent would ever have been good enough for more than hack work. His ideas were mostly for narrative drawing and caricature, and even those were aborted by the needle of Christine's impatience. He would not dare to produce paint boxes or sketch pads in front of her. He tried to write novels: it was a less noticeable activity for a man whose profession involved a good deal of note-taking. Two books were in the hands of his agent now, though, she had been obliged to tell him, much rejected. They both still cherished hopes for them. Meanwhile the law for the kids provided her with a bit of cash to be going along with.

But it was neither the novels nor the slim published work which had transformed Mike Roper's life during the last few years. It was the discovery, years too late, that the freedoms of a permissive society extended to people like himself. He wasted years envying younger and bolder men the pleasures which he had assumed to be illicit for the generation whose youth had been spent on saving and studying, on bettering itself. Suddenly Jack was as good as his master, and Mike realised that he was not the master. The humblest articled clerk in his office—a figure of speech, in fact, since he had only one articled clerk, who was arrogant—was better and happier than the Mike Roper who slaved for his undeserving clients and unappreciative wife. The world was full of the poor, who were rich in pleasure. He could not remember later whether this revelation crept up on him or came in a flash. It appeared in its full glory, he thought, on the day that a temporary typist met his eyes as he made his usual surreptitious appraisal,

7

and pulled her skirt a little higher up her legs, and her shoulders back to display her breasts. She was the first one; since then there had been a girl usher at one of the magistrate's courts, someone's Danish au pair girl, another solicitor's articled clerk, and his agent's secretary. From her his agent had acquired the image of Mike as an obsessive sleeper-around; she knew that Mike liked to be introduced to girls, and acted on the principle of keeping her own clients happy.

At the Palfrey & Blackwood party she was cornered at the far end of the room, and Mike was stuck with two old, unloved acquaintances. At the last event of this kind, where he had first met them, he had invented a formula: the younger the reader, the older the writer. Emily Bromley, who had just published *Wild Willie's Warren*, was eighty if she was a day, and wore a pink net hat. Nancy Megarry, of *Felicity and the Forest Fire*, was a hearty, tweedy fifty.

Mike edged his way towards a waiter, and was joined there by his agent. She shrugged her shoulders a little apologetically and said, 'Not much talent, I'm afraid.' He was staring at a pretty blonde and she added, 'That's no good. She's engaged to John Blackwood.'

Mike moved on to look at some of the firm's publications which were displayed on the side tables. His own book, with some idealised children holding the scales of justice on the cover, was half-concealed by a thicker volume with a picture of two entwined bodies on it. It was called *A Pleasure to Come* by Jane Shore. He wondered whether Palfrey & Blackwood could really have meant what it said. He picked up the book and was startled on the first page he looked at by a kind of frankness he had always supposed only men could put on paper, an explicit feminine description which for a moment disgusted before it excited him. He glanced around, embarrassed at his own reaction.

'Mike.' A heavy hand clapped him on the shoulder. 'Good to see you. My dear chap, we're doing splendidly with your opus. I expect you know lots of people here.' John Blackwood was a professional host. 'Ah, I see you're looking at one of our newest works—have you met Jane Shore? I'm sure you'd—ah, Miss Shore. Let me introduce—' He completed the formalities and gracefully left them together. She had dark hair which she fingered as though it made her uneasy. She was wearing a black dress without jewellery, and looked smart but not fashionable. She must know that any man who had seen her book would be wondering whether it was fact or fantasy, and seemed shy. A nerve at the corner of her mouth twitched just visibly.

'Do you come to this sort of thing often?' he asked.

'Never in my life,' she said, smiling.

'Oh, is this your first book?'

'Yes.'

The party was thinning out by this time. He could see, looking over Jane Shore's head, that there were no prettier girls in the room.

Mike's agent sidled up to him, and whispered, 'Just wanted to say goodbye, darling. I must fly. So glad you're fixed up.' A kiss landed on his ear; she was one of the few women whom Mike liked and had never fancied. Jane Shore looked shy; she glanced around the room and said, 'I suppose I'd better be off. It's so nice to have—'

'Come and eat, won't you?' he interrupted. 'Or are you fixed up?'

'I—well, no. Thank you very much, I'd like to.' She followed him to say goodbye to John Blackwood, who shook her hand and said he was glad to have met her, and that she must come to London again soon, and always drop in at Palfrey & Blackwood when she did. He winked

9

at Mike behind her back, but more as though it was his habit than as if he was hinting anything. Mike wondered where to go for dinner. He wasn't sure how much money she was worth. Though perhaps for a short time ... but she was not his usual type. He went more for girls who dressed casually and had wild hair; that seemed to be their badge of availability. Was it worth spending the money on a good dinner, he was wondering, when she came towards him looking luscious in a floor-length fur coat. He instantly decided on a French restaurant in Charlotte Street.

The conversation was uncomfortably polite, both in the taxi and as they ate hors d'oeuvres and fish. Mike had admitted to being a solicitor and living in Ealing; he had discovered that Jane Shore lived in the country and she mentioned a husband and two children in passing. She was completely unlike the usual sort of girl he took out to dinner, and he enjoyed listening to her high voice with what he thought of as a 'God damn you' accent. She made no effort to lower it in public; that, however, was the rule at this sort of restaurant, which was full of middle-class couples expressing their certainties. Only Mike, whose voice did not match his neighbours', lowered it as he spoke. And in the far corner of the room, a famous actor was quietly eating and ignoring the covert glances which the other diners directed at him. Jane had started the conversation with the usual queries about Mike's work, and spurious declarations of interest in it. He could just hear her, he thought, at cocktail parties, saying, 'What do you do?' to each man she met. No doubt she asked women which public school their children had been put down for. But as the claret followed the Chablis and the publisher's sherry, she relaxed the formality.

Her face grew flushed, and her carefully set hair slid from its moorings. At the crème caramel stage Mike said,

'You'll sleep with me afterwards, will you?'

'What? Sorry, I thought you said—'

'Yes, I did. I've got a bed at my office. You'll come back there?'

She stared at him, her mouth open. Her lipstick had rubbed off, and the silver paint on her eyelids had formed a tiny ridge along the crease. Her cheeks were flushed pink, and her forehead shining. She looked unsure of herself and astonished. Mike watched her mind and then her lips forming an automatic offended refusal, and her hands feeling for her bag. She pushed her feet under the chair, and was about to scrape it backwards and make a dignified departure. Suddenly she relaxed, and ran the tip of her tongue across her lips.

'Why do you—?'

'You're very attractive,' he said, staring at her bosom.

'I—well, all right. Yes, I will.' She sat back as though she were exhausted by her own boldness, and Mike summoned the bill before she could change her mind. In the taxi he held her hand, but hers lay flaccid in his, and she sat at the other end of the seat, looking at him when she thought he would not notice. He wondered what he had let himself in for, and decided that at his time of life he could not be bothered with modesty and deception. He hoped she would not sit up afterwards and ask, 'What must you think of me?'

But his apprehension was misplaced. He gave her some brandy as soon as they entered the room, and she stripped off her clothes and leapt under the covers without hesitation, and proceeded to astonish him with her energy. His first touch of her skin seemed, as it were, to galvanise her, but though ardent, she was inexpert. She smoked as though she were not used to that either, when they lay back with more brandy afterwards. He saw her looking around the small dirty room.

11

Mike's office consisted of the top two floors of a shabby house in a shabby street. On the ground floor was a shop selling newspapers and girlie magazines; the first-floor offices were occupied by a travel agency which dealt only in cheap tickets to the Caribbean and India. At least half the residents in the immediate neighbourhood, and nearly three-quarters of Mike's clients, were immigrants. He had set up his own plate after working for a couple of years in one of the first free legal advice centres. His offices had been those of a drunken old solicitor who survived on small conveyancing work for fifty years, going downhill with the neighbourhood. Mike lived off payments from the Law Society for legal aid work. He was just able to afford a typist and a rather inferior articled clerk, but would never be able to keep up more than the small flat in Ealing to which Christine contributed as much as he.

On one floor he had his own office and the typist's room, into which the front door opened; each room could just hold a smallish desk and one extra chair. In the two rooms above all the filing cabinets and other equipment were crammed; in one the articled clerk was supposed to sit, when he bothered to turn up. In the other there was just room for a divan bed. It was officially for the typist and for female clients, in case any of them 'came over queer'. He had claimed, when it arrived, that he was merely complying with the provisions of the Shops and Offices Act, and he doubted whether either of his employees would have bothered to check the statute. In any case, he made no secret, to them or to anyone much, of what the bed was really for. He was proud to have discovered licence. He had bought the bed in a sale, bouncing enjoyably with the young woman assistant until the dust flew and the supervisor came to stop them. He had a black fitted sheet on the mattress, which he occasionally took to the laundry, and there was an uncovered continental quilt and some foam rubber pillows which a girl who was allergic to feathers had provided.

The lavatory was shared with the other tenants and was on the first floor, but he had a cold-water tap in the typist's room, and a cupboard containing instant coffee and milk powder and an electric kettle. He kept the brandy bottle in one of the metal box files, where the typist would not look. The cleaner was an immense West Indian woman, who was supposed to come in every day at eight. In fact she turned up about three times a week in the middle of the morning and pushed some of the dust from one surface to another after drinking a lot of sweet coffee and scattering more biscuit than she ever swept up. There were mouse droppings in all the corners.

Jane's face was expressionless as she glanced at the small cracked window, which looked out, at this level, on another roof with wooden battens showing through the gaps in the slates. There was a small courtyard at ground level, where waste-paper flapped in large, inexplicably oily puddles. She glanced from the ceiling, bubbled with damp, to the string backing which showed through the worn linoleum. Her clothes had smeared marks in the dust as she threw them on to the grey metal filing cabinets.

'Have you ever done this before?' he asked.

'I told you,' she said, 'I'm married. I've got two children.'

He wondered about even the brief passage in her book which he had had time to read. Its lascivious prose had not matched her performance, in his opinion. He said, 'I meant sleeping with someone else. Committing adultery.' She did not answer, and he said, almost triumphantly, 'I do believe you never did. You must be unique.'

'How could you tell? There's nothing—'

'No, no, you're fine. Great. It's just that you don't seem—'

'Well, I must say that I am a bit surprised to find myself sitting up here beside you,' she admitted. 'It must be all that booze.' He thought, Now she'll be all contrite. But she went on, 'What a waste. Now I've taken the step I can't think why I never did before.' She took a swig of the brandy. 'It's much nicer out of matrimony. I've always envied my swinging sister this kind of life, and now I see that I was quite right.'

He thought, Wait till you're sober, my girl, you're the kind to get remorse, and confess all.

'Where are we, anyway?' she asked. 'I didn't notice, somehow, on the way.'

'At my office. What did you think?'

'Well, but I meant the address. For next time. Don't you want there to be a next time? Aren't I—?'

'Yes, of course I do,' he said quickly. 'But I thought you said you didn't live in London. I mean, if your home is a long way—where do you live?'

'Oh, miles away. But I can come again. There's always something—dentists—doctors—'

Mascara had made black smudges below her eyes, but she was rosy and her eyes were sparkling. She looked distinctly sexy. Momentarily he wondered about the husband, presumably a poor fish since he had taught her so little; perhaps he was imprisoned in the archaic chastity from which Mike had so triumphantly freed himself. It would be doing a favour to the chap to teach his Jane what it was all about; he saw a design in his mind, a two-dimensional way to express the idea he had just had of a continuous chain of amatory instruction, from lover to spouse to lover to spouse.... He pulled her down on top of him again, thinking with pleasure of red-faced executives in the Shores' part of the stockbroker belt, meeting a new, oncoming and sexy Jane at their expensive parties. 'Oy, oy, what's up with her then?' they would think, and then, no doubt, accept what was offered. He liked the idea of sending an unsuspected changeling back to Mr Shore's unadventurous arms.

Jane came to London again. She was not unwelcome. For she was available and willing, and the fact was that he had not been able to replace his last girl, who went to America, as easily as he had expected. Possibly there were girls in London who wanted the rolls in the hay without boring emotional complications, but it was not so easy to find them. He certainly didn't want them to fall in love with him and want him to surrender Samantha—for that was what leaving Christine would mean. It was a sobering realisation. Somewhere in London there were the gorgeous girls who would leap as casually into his bed and out of it again as his reading and his imagination had made him suppose. But he'd been deceiving himself, when he said they came his way.

He felt a little surprised, as the summer went on, by how little Jane revealed of herself. He knew no more than on the day they met about her home or family. He did not even know her husband's first name. At first he had been relieved to be spared, for girls sometimes exacted sympathetic listening as their charge for what they let him have, and he had occasionally wondered whether women endured the part he enjoyed, for the sake of lying back afterwards and telling him all the minutiae of their lives. He had learnt to be careful not to ask anything that might encourage them to think he wished to know.

Perversity made him wonder about Jane, merely because she had told him nothing. And he was surprised too by her lack of interest in the surroundings where they met. A woman from her putative background ought, he thought, to care about domestic details. Why did she not, for instance, dust the filing cabinets with a paper handkerchief, as one of his girls had done, or, like another, bring fresh linen for the bed? Jane even left Mike to make the coffee and pour the brandy. She would lie naked on the soiled sheet, engulfed in squalor, and indifferent to it. From all she said to the contrary she would have been happy to meet him and part from him there without ever knowing him any better. Was it possible that she was only interested in him in bed? Having embarked upon the affair determined that there only would she interest him, Mike was provoked by her matching his intention. It was he who began to suggest expeditions to cinemas and parks; it was he who acquired a miniature cooking ring and began to bring food for them to share. It was he whom she allowed to clear it up.

Mike had the only key to his office so that he knew they were safe from interruption. They used to meet there at six, after the staff had gone. Once or twice she came on a Saturday, and he suggested leaving the dingy attic and going out together.

'Don't you ever worry that someone you know might see you?' he asked her once.

'You can't imagine how unlikely it is,' she said. They were in the National Gallery at the time. It was July and there had been a queue to get in, and gaggles of students and tourists blocked the view of all the best-known paintings. Jane and Mike sat on a slippery leather bench, designed to let art lovers take the weight off their feet without encouraging them to settle in comfort. Jane pointed to the picture they were facing, Gainsborough's pastoral portrait of Mr and Mrs Robert Andrews. 'That's the world I live in,' she said. 'That could be me and—my husband.'

'Oh come on. What is his name, anyway? You've never mentioned it.'

'You never asked.'

'Well, I'm asking.'

'I don't think I'll tell you,' she said. 'It's rather nice to

16

keep it all separate. I like leading a double life.'

'Is that what Mr Shore looks like, then? The woman isn't a bit like you.'

'No, he doesn't really. We're not so pop-eyed. But look at them, so prosperous, so bored, so respectable. I bet they were married off by their relations without a word of argument.'

'Is that what happened to you?'

'Of course not. We were desperately in love,' she said, twinkling at him. 'But we sit on the edge of cornfields and admire the crop. He even carries a gun when we go for walks if it's the right time of the year.'

'And the dog too?'

'Yes, only it's a retriever!'

'It doesn't fit in with my picture of the way you live,' he said. 'Have you got all those rolling acres?' He'd imagined her in rich suburbia. She put her hand in his, and nuzzled his cheek with her face.

'Don't look so embarrassed,' she said. 'I should think we're the only English people in this building except for the attendants.' He watched a pair of girls walk uninterestedly through the room, their high, round bottoms tightly outlined by their jeans. They were wearing an international uniform, but Jane said, 'Look at those French girls. Isn't it funny how you can always tell? Something to do with their Bardot pouts, I think.'

'Where do you live, anyway?' he said. He had not been interested, until it was becoming obvious that Jane did not want him to know.

'I told you, in the country. Surrounded by dogs and cats and ducks and ponies and cows and sheep and pigs and—'

'I've been out of London, thanks,' he said.

'Oh, well, then you know what it's like. It's terribly dull. I'm just a housewife. I don't want to spoil your regard for me by explaining how prosaic my home life is.' He

17

wondered whether to tell her that her prosaic and conventional married life had been made clear the first time he had her in bed. They got up, and strolled on. 'It's nice, isn't it,' she said, 'looking at pictures together? I haven't been here since I was at school.'

'Did you go to school in London?'

'Yes, I did. I can still remember how embarrassing it was to march through here in a crocodile of girls. I used to dream about escaping to some desert island. I imagined it like the picture by a Dutch painter—come on, I'll show you.' She took his hand and he followed her to stand in front of a smallish landscape painting which was, the label said, thought to be the only surviving fragment of a larger scene. Chalky rocks rose from ideally smooth turquoise water, matched by white clouds in a blue sky. 'I used to lose myself in that. It's so unrealistic, and yet seemed so possible. Actually, I suppose it would be like that in Greece or somewhere. Don't you wish we were somewhere like that, Mike? Wouldn't it be lovely if we could just go away somewhere, and lie and make love in the sun?'

After that day in the gallery, she had been particularly passionate in bed. She had stopped being shy about letting him see her naked. She was no longer ashamed for him to see stretch marks and bulges: this time she exhausted him by the nude gymnastics, and by her energetic putting into practice of the tricks he had taught her. Was that the day that he had started to be afraid that he was going to love her?

It was a hard summer in his practice. He was kept inordinately busy, but did not seem to make even as much money as he used to, let alone more. Christine did not fail to let him know that housekeeping required more money to keep at the same standard; Samantha was begging to go on a school excursion to Normandy; his agent sent back one of his two novels saying that she had given up hope of being able to place it. He re-read it one Sunday, shut up in his bedroom in the flat, and knew that it was good. He had written about a solicitor whose compassion for humanity, which had taken him into a social service type of practice, did not stand up to the real-life clients he encountered, and who was forced to enter a local authority's legal advice department where he would be able to do good to the needy without having to meet them. It was a valid point he was making; he was sure it needed saying. He was proud that he had not written the autobiographical first novel, and wondered whether even his agent realised that the book represented the very opposite of his own emotions.

Mike could only recognise the reality of a social problem, homelessness for instance, when he saw its victims; his indignation against the cruelty of modern life only flourished when the wretched client was in his own office. But he grew increasingly depressed by the intransigence of the problems and the intractability of the clients. What could he do, for instance, about Mrs O'Leary, whose husband drank his wages and beat her on Saturdays, but whose religion would allow her to take no steps against him or the perpetual child-bearing he inflicted upon her? Or about Mrs Williams from Jamaica whose son Ezekiel had been picked up by the police for borrowing a bike, and been in trouble ever since? His original offence would have merited only a ticking off from his dad if he had been a middle-class child, but Mrs Williams watched her son sliding further and further into crime with a helpless fatalism. What could he do for old Mr and Mrs Cunningham, who were being evicted by the council from the terraced cottage they had lived in for fifty-two years? They knew and he knew that central heating and a wide view from the eighteenth floor would kill them both in two years. Who could help Zeba Pradesh, who had been left with three children and a rigid sense of pride which drove her to earn by working as a night nurse, convinced that the children were safe in their sleep? One day they would die in a fire or kill themselves in another of the countless childish accidents. But how else could she earn enough to keep them? Sometimes in the night he felt that he was like the seven maids with seven mops trying to sweep the beach clean. There was indeed no end to the problems people asked him to solve, which he could hardly mitigate.

To think, he thought, how he had slaved to qualify himself for this job.

Mike's father, who had been killed in the Second World War, was the son of a farm labourer; he and Marjorie Sawley had met when she was on a works outing in his part of the world. It was hard to believe that they had been happy together, the girl from an industrial town and a man chained by tradition to the soil. Mike sometimes wondered whether the few years they had together could have been the idyll which his mother chose to remember. What about the mud, the labour, the loneliness? But Marjorie went home to her mother with small Mike, and her husband was killed in North Africa. She sometimes wept still to think of the alien sand which engulfed a body reared on the cold clay of the Essex marshes.

Mike was brought up by his mother and his grandmother in a small flat above a corner shop in Reading. He was constantly admonished to better himself, and constantly told at school that he could better himself if he tried. His grandmother made a bugbear of the slog and boredom that would be his lot in either farm or factory. But his mother's absent-minded disdain for the work of running the shop had even more influence on him. Her attitude made it clear that the kind of work she did to keep him could be no ambition for a man. Somewhere at the back of his mind he'd had the idea of returning to the country. He used to search his consciousness for a race memory of the land, but was unmoved by the plants his mother nurtured in a back-yard and uncomfortable on their day trips to the Chilterns. Anyway, there was no future in farming for boys like him, he knew that without ever mentioning the subject at home. So it was scholarships to school and university; assistance through articles in a city firm of solicitors; and a revulsion at the end of his period of training against the impersonal commercial clients he had learnt to deal with, and the family trusts, and the million-pound deals. He welcomed the chance to cope with what he thought of as real people with real problems in a neighbourhood legal advice centre, and left it to set up on his own only because he didn't get on with his colleagues. He resented the way they gave a false impression of being working class and all in it together with their clients. He was the only one of them who really came from a poor background, and he acted a different part.

Mike's mother and grandmother died in the same year and the shop in Reading was sold. As the years went by he found that he never remembered it as his home. There was an impression deep within him of another home altogether, so vague as not to include a house or even a room; it was just of a field, a corner of a field, where there were green hedges and some elm trees, and some thin grass, with a cow pat on it and a ragged pink flower in the hedge. He must have been in a field like that on one of those Sunday bus trips to the Berkshire countryside, when he was very small; perhaps even before, when he lived—as he had done until the age of three—in the Essex home of his ancestors. He always meant to go and look for it one day. But Christine did not like the country.

Mike was almost embarrassed to remember in what corny circumstances he had met Christine. She had even said, when they were engaged, that it was just like a story in *Woman's Own*. But she had been proud of the likeness. Mike had sprained his ankle when he was running for a bus and it had to be X-rayed. Christine had been the assistant radiographer and they had started going out together and sleeping together very casually. He had never known a coloured girl well before. At his school and colleges students had made friends in their own class and racial groups, and he now noticed that even at the age of four Samantha repeated the same pattern. Her best friend was the coffee-coloured daughter of a Pakistani doctor and a nurse from Leicester. Not that Samantha was coffee-coloured herself, and Mike's deepest, most secret shame, amongst many, was that he was glad of her likeness to himself. Christine had taken after her mother and she looked purely Indian, though her voice was native London and so had her education and outlook been.

They had been very happy at first. He could never quite remember when she started being intolerant of his preoccupations and scornful of his attitudes. But he was sure that she despised him before he disliked her. She said that he was dishonest and he that she was unimaginative; they lived together, they said, for Samantha.

In the autumn Mike began to take an early-closing day, like his neighbours in the shops. Jane had said it was becoming difficult to get away from home at weekends, and he wanted to see her for more than the odd evening. Their meetings were unsatisfactory, for she did a horrible Cinderella act, rushing off to catch a train when he was still lying somnolent and sated and would have liked to spin the time out. She would never let him come with her to the station, but insisted on catching the underground train. After a while he realised that it was because she did not wish him to know where she was going.

Sometimes she was able to stay on a little while and they would cook a meal on the single electric ring. He taught her to boil eggs in a kettle, and to acquire the eggs without paying for them. He was so skilful that even Jane, beside him, only realised what he was doing when her exclamation would have been disastrous, but he stood on her foot in time to stop her. She was wearing, as he was, a pair of jeans and a sweater which she stored in one of the drawers of a filing cabinet. Her suit was folded on top of it, waiting for her to reassume her other personality. They both wore dirty tennis shoes and he was able to grind her instep so painfully that she forgot to say, in a penetrating middle-class voice, 'Oh, look, you put these in the wrong bag.' But she was aghast at the omission. Only the fact that messy couples quarrelling on the pavement were a common sight in the High Street protected them from particular notice, but he managed to get her back into the office before she had betrayed him.

Mike was surprised at her reaction to what had become his normal procedure. She jumped as though she had been sitting on a hot griddle when he mentioned, in the argument, that he had got even the sheet she was sitting on in the same way. She kept repeating 'But you can't, really you mustn't. And you a solicitor!'

'I don't see what that's got to do with it,' he said. He began to break the stolen eggs into the saucepan, and produced a small tin of anchovies from his pocket.

'Well, but Mike—an officer of the court! A commissioner for oaths! I don't see how—'

'Words, words. **Guff.**'

'But Mike—'

'Do stop saying "But Mike" and come here!' He reached out to her but she pushed him away.

'It's wrong. You know it as well as I do. Stealing!'

'Save that for your kids.'

'How can you be so—'

'Look, Jane. Do you know who I see here, in this office, day after bloody day? Do you know who they are, the people who come and sit round here? Do you know how they live? Have you ever been to a prison and seen the people that get put away for less than your posh friends do every time they sell a share or a stock or something? And if I don't condemn my clients, why should I be any better than them? It's meaningless to worry about the odd box of eggs. Everyone does it if they can get away with it. Honestly.'

'Honestly! I think you're mad.'

'I'm not mad.' He pulled her to sit down beside him on the bed. 'Listen, Jane, nearly twenty years now I've worked in this sort of practice. You think they're different from you, the prostitutes and thieves and murderers and pimps

24

and baby bashers and abortionists—don't you? You think you're better, more honest, hard working, deserving, you think they are the dregs of society, you think it's their fault. Don't you? People like you, the ones on top, the person I might have been. But they aren't.'

'No, I don't—'

'Oh yes you do. You may only think so subconsciously, I'll grant you that. But deep down inside you, there is that certainty, you wouldn't have been like that, no pressures would have moulded you into what you call crime, what people like you have defined as crime. Well, I'm on their side. Not just because I'm paid to be, the miserable pittance the state lets me have for representing people who can't afford to buy better law, but because I'm like them. The ones at the bottom of the pile.'

'But I still don't understand why you—after all, it's not as though you can't afford—'

'No, but why should I? It's my gesture. I do it on principle. I'm waving my flag.'

They made love, and her face was mutinous and disapproving, but she was more excited than he had ever known her. And the next time they went shopping she wore a dress and had her hair combed. She could have got away with anything in that rig, and when they were in the room again she produced a small jar of ginger and some ice cream wafers from her handbag with an expression on her face both gleeful and guilty.

'I must say it was rather fun,' she admitted. 'The adrenalin flowed.'

'I'm corrupting you.'

'Yes, aren't you?' she smiled, more for herself than for him. 'A new woman; a different me. Whatever next!'

Jane progressed, in fact, unprodded by Mike. She started bringing him presents, not wrapped in the shop's paper, produced proudly, like a cat with a new kitten;

she brought him a tie with a label of a shop in Bond Street, a pot of Stilton cheese from Fortnum & Mason, some rare cigarettes, and he teased her about the shops she frequented.

One day in November she came with something he did not recognise. A mild damp day; he stood to the side of the front window, hoping to see her hurrying along from the underground station. The streets below him were crowded with anxious, tired shoppers. Jane arrived in a taxi like a visitor from a gilded world.

After they had made love she said she wanted to ask him a favour.

'Depends what,' he said.

'Well, I wanted to sell something. I need some money— what I got from Palfrey & Blackwood hasn't gone as far as I expected—all those train fares! But I'm a bit shy about going to a shop myself. I thought perhaps you could—'

'What is it?'

'Well, I don't suppose it's all that valuable. Look.' She leant over the side of the bed and pulled her handbag up. It was ludicrous to see this dishevelled woman holding a crocodile-skin bag, opening the gilt clasp with an automatic gesture of her red nails, and rummaging within it. He laughed.

'You don't know how comic you look,' he said. 'Let me see.' There were ragged letters and old bills and Green Shield stamps, muddled up with a shagreen cigarette case, and a matching set of powder compact and lipstick. A slim wallet fell on to the bed and he picked it up. On the corner was a gilt initial V.

'What's it stand for?' he said.

'What—oh. The letter V. It stands for Vera. That's my mother's name. Here, let me put it back.'

'No, let me look. What funny things you keep in your

bag. A recipe for egg mousse and a mail-order form for children's life jackets. What sort of life do you lead at home, my poor Jane? A premium bond certificate and train ticket for—'

'Don't be silly. Let me have that, and you look at this.' She handed him a little package of tissue paper, which he unwrapped, and he let the contents fall upon the bed.

'I don't know a thing about Chinese art,' he said. 'Is this valuable?'

'I should think it must be quite. But I really can't see myself being very dynamic with a dealer. If you were to ...'

'That's all very well, but he'd probably think I'd pinched it.'

'I don't see why. Not if you wear a suit, anyway. The one you wear in court. Just say it was in your family, you inherited it. Your great-grandfather brought it back from a world tour.'

'Is that what your great-grandfather did?'

'Sort of.'

'Is there lots more where that came from?' She did not answer, but started to take off her clothes in a businesslike way. She had never learnt to provoke and thrill him as she undressed; it was like watching a wife getting ready for bed, undramatic and comfortable. Was that the moment when she first seemed like Christine? He watched as she rolled her tights down, and frowned at a small hole, and licked her finger before rubbing it over the thin fabric. She shook her pants neatly and folded them on top of her other clothes, indifferent to his eyes on her body. There was a red line around her waist from the elastic. Her legs were slightly stubbly, for she was no longer as meticulous about preparing herself for their meetings as she had been, but instead of annoying him, the evidence of her familiar, casual attitude excited him. He was suddenly divided by two emotions, wanting this arrangement to go on for ever, and wanting to change it into a different one. He thought it would be good to live with her, to know what she was like at breakfast and when she was ill, to hear her making grocery lists and grumbling about sewing on buttons.

Mike got far more money than he expected for the Chinese figure. He had not wanted to sell it anywhere near his home or his office, for a man in his profession was recognised by far more people than he knew, and to have such a thing was completely out of character for him. What on earth, he wondered, would Christine make of it? The ornaments in their flat, chosen by her, but admired by them both, were raffia dolls, flimsy glass animals which matched nothing in the world's fauna, lamps with tropical shells stuck on their stands, and a pair of wooden vases which they had brought back from a holiday in Yugoslavia, decorated with a hot poker and not watertight. He did not like the Chinese buffalo, but could see that it was the kind of thing museums would display. Perhaps, he thought, Jane lived in the kind of house furnished with glass tables full of delicate objects, and corner cupboards, and painted plates on wire stands, and silver ashtrays and cigarette boxes. He had occasionally entered such houses when he was an articled clerk, visiting clients with his principal, so that he could witness their wills and documents.

The shop he finally chose was near the British Museum. Its window was full of ivory statues and thin porcelain bowls. It amused him to realise how often he must have glanced unseeing at such displays, never noticing what they were. The things people waste their money on, he thought. He expected to get about a fiver for the buffalo, and would have given as many pence for it himself.

A middle-aged man and woman were discussing a purchase with the only person behind the counter, who was stroking it, a white jar of no more charm that Mike could see than a milk bottle. They mentioned patina and glaze and firing, and dynasties with unrepeatable pronunciations. Eventually the jar was paid for and meticulously wrapped, and the couple left the shop with expressions of esteem on either side. Mike wondered what on earth they would do with the pot now they had it; they could hardly stick daffodils in something which had cost them a three-figure sum.

'Do you buy as well as sell?' Mike asked.

'Sometimes.' The man behind the counter looked cautiously at Mike, and rested his hands on the glass counter. In the display cabinet beneath it were various pieces of carved stone which looked quite like the one in Mike's pocket, and he took it out and laid it on the square of green baize.

'I don't suppose it's of much value,' he said. 'Just something my grandfather brought home. He was a great traveller. Clutters up the house, you know.' The other man picked the buffalo up and held it close to his eyes. He had dirty hands, but held the little figure delicately. He breathed deeply and slowly, and the black hairs on the back of his fingers were blown to and fro. He looked over his semicircular spectacles at Mike.

'How much do you want for it?'

'I'm not sure. What would you say would be—?'

'I couldn't offer more than forty-five.' He put it down, as though he expected Mike to snatch it away, outraged.

'Forty-five? Well—'

'I suppose you might get more from someone else. I'm a little over-stocked at the moment.'

'You don't seem very keen to buy,' Mike said.

'Oh, I'll take it, I'll take it. It's quite nice. If you'll accept my price.'

'Done.'

'I ought to ask—normal practice—evidence of ownership—a little embarrassing. . . .' Under the straggling beard was a faint reddening.

'My dear sir,' Mike spoke in his plummiest voice, the one he had developed when he was in articles. 'Of course. I'm a solicitor myself—commendable caution.'

'Oh well, sir, if you're a lawyer that's all right. It's just—you know how it is.'

'Say no more.' Mike put his briefcase on the counter. 'See for yourself.'

'Oh no, sir. No need for that. I'll just—' He counted the money out in one-pound notes, which he drew from a bulging wallet. Mike shoved them in his jacket pocket without counting them, and the proprietor came round to hold the door open for him. Mike walked along Russell Street with his hand in his pocket, fingering the money. If he had been offered forty-five pounds, the buffalo must have been worth at least sixty to the shop owner and would probably be sold for ninety. Jane had given it to him as though it mattered to her no more than her lipstick. There was probably not a single object in Mike and Christine's flat which would be worth as much as twenty pounds at a sale. Even the television set was on hire, and the washing machine was eight years old and was more often broken than not. Forty-five pounds for that lump of snot-coloured stone!

He wondered whether Jane would be as surprised at its value as he was, but she accepted the money without comment. She said in fact, he uneasily felt, less and less. At the beginning of their relationship he had been bored to think of the advance payment of conversation and attention he would have to put down, in the hope of receiving her favours. Now he found himself thinking about her when she was not there and looking forward to her arrival. He wanted to understand the life of which he had hardly an inkling; how did she live with that husband and those children, what did she do in her rural fastness? But now that he wanted to know she evaded his questions. He feared that she thought his discussion a defilement, that by telling him she would sully them. As the plan grew in his mind to make his relationship with her permanent, to become the centre not the fringe of her life, so Jane grew less and less forthcoming. She said that she did not want to talk about her home, why didn't they just enjoy the moment while it lasted? And he sensed a silent abstraction if he talked about himself; yet he wanted to tell her his life, he wanted her sympathy; he was determined that she should take an interest in Samantha, as a preparation to—well, he admitted to himself, to living with her.

He thought of the times they had been together; so few, when he reckoned them up. From the autumn when he met her, through the winter to the spring, how many times? Not more than nine or ten. He waited for her at his upstairs window, watching the life in the street below. The market stalls offered daffodils and tulips. He wondered whether Jane lived surrounded by flowers at home. Perhaps she had a garden full of cherry trees and herbaceous borders. He pictured her in a floppy straw hat, with a loose cream-coloured dress, in the middle of a smooth lawn with children and dogs gambolling around her. He had read her book several times by now. The sexy bits rang even less true than he had thought when he glanced through them at Palfrey & Blackwood's party. She was not a bit like that in bed herself. Once he quoted some of her own words to her as she lay spreadeagled below him; she pushed him away.

'Stop it!' she exclaimed. 'You don't understand.'

He felt deeply tender towards her. 'Darling, never mind. I understand. You don't have to pretend with me.'

'What are you talking about?'

'That it was your fantasies. Orgies of the country mouse. But it's better in real life, isn't it? Your heroine was a bit sick, actually.'

'All you mean is that you like it straight,' she said.

'Don't you?'

'Mmm.' Was their embrace a little mechanical? Did she really want him to expand the scope of their intimacies? But she pushed him away when he attempted untried refinements. 'It wasn't autobiography,' she said. 'I like it straight too.'

It could not have been Jane's own life story, that much Mike was sure was true. *A Pleasure to Come* was the tale, funny and moving, Palfrey & Blackwood's blurb writer had written, of the amorous adventures of a rich young wife who lived in a mansion somewhere by the sea. Her encounters took place variously in her drawing-rooms, attics and stables, once on the scullery table, and in the last scene in a Chinese-style folly which dominated her famous garden. The heroine's acrobatic encounter with a sailor took place near its pinnacle. There was not much plot, but plenty of action, described with a mixture of Anglo-Saxon frankness and lush metaphor. Mike had preferred the four-letter words to the purple passages. 'Dazzling mouths, inexorable tides, earthquakes and exploding stars' struck him as false notes to describe any of his own sensations; nor, he felt certain, did the earth ever move for Jane. He was the first to admit that he had no qualifications as a literary critic. The last novel he had read for fun before *A Pleasure to Come* was *The Cruel Sea*. But he would have sworn that Jane had written down her wilder fantasies and they had been published as high-class porn. That might explain, he supposed, why she was apparently ashamed to discuss it.

Easter was at the end of April. Christine had insisted on making the holidays for a change, and she and Mike were to take Samantha to Wales. Mike did not want to go, but Christine's mother who usually looked after Samantha during the school holidays was not well and Christine had no choice but to take her three weeks in the spring. As she acidly remarked, Mike was not after all willing to let the child hang around the office making herself useful to the secretary, which would have been perfectly possible. Whatever Christine did irritated Mike now. Even when she cooked him a supper he liked, without asking for his help or grumbling when he did not offer it, he felt that she could do nothing right. Somewhere ahead, he confidently hoped, lay a halcyon new life, with Jane, and Samantha, and a cottage and a field, and the easy life of a country lawyer who had time to dig his own garden. In the summer he intended to start househunting in Essex or Suffolk.

Jane came a fortnight before Easter, saying that she would not be back for a while as her school holidays also tended to be child-bound. She produced something else for Mike to sell, an even odder object, he thought, than the last. It was an enamel egg, riotously yet delicately decorated in blues and greens, with a gilt rim and hinge opening to reveal an oddly shaped, padded velvet hollow inside.

'It's a Fabergé Easter Egg,' she said. 'Russian. I suppose you would have to know that much if you're going to pretend it's yours to sell.'

'Russian? I shouldn't think the shop I went to would do for it then. Not that it would be sensible to go back. Is this the sort of thing that would be easy to—well, do people want enamel Easter Eggs?'

'I'm sure that lots do. It ought to be worth as much as the Chinese buffalo. Try somewhere in Bond Street. Or Kensington. Lots of suitable shops in Church Street, at least there used to be.'

They lay on their backs staring at the cracked ceiling. Mike had taught Jane to blow smoke rings, and she puffed wispy haloes into the air. Mike laid his arm across her body and rested his hand on her thigh. He savoured the softness of her breast which rested against him, free falling where other girls on his bed had been upstanding. He loved the maturity he felt in her. In Christine, age had roughened and experience hardened what in Jane remained vulnerable both physically and metaphorically.

'I don't want you to go away,' he said.

'That's nice of you.'

'I mean it. Stay with me, Jane. We'll be so happy.'

'Love in a garret.'

'No, seriously. Listen, Jane, let's stick together. Wouldn't you like it too? We could move to the country, East Anglia might be the place, take your children and Samantha, get married.'

'Love in a cottage.'

'Yes, I suppose it would be that. I'd like to get back to the country. My ancestors were on the land.'

'I must go.' She rolled herself off the bed, and stood unselfconsciously naked, dishevelled and no longer perfect either where nature or art had made her so. He said,

'Jane, I love you. I want you. I know you didn't think I did. I've been a bastard, letting you give me everything without— But I love you too now. We'll be so happy.'

She pulled her tights on quickly, and a controlling pair of knickers over them, which left the flesh of her thighs to bulge on either side below where the elastic cut into her flesh. Her petticoat was greyish, but smelt of her scent. 'Think about it. We can grow our own vegetables. Have bees perhaps. Have some more children.' Christine had been told she must never have any more after Samantha's birth, and had recently had a hysterectomy.

Jane propped her open compact on the filing cabinet, and bent to see her face while she retouched the make-up. She wore a black coat, and looked unapproachable and

34

strange. Mike jumped out of the bed, and stood behind her, pressing himself hard against her. 'Come back soon. Think about what I said.'

She gave him a brief smile, and the sort of cheek-to-cheek kiss she might have given a girl-friend.

'Goodbye,' she said. 'I must go. Goodbye.' He leaned out over the banisters as she hurried down the stairs.

'You'll let me know next time? We'll do it, won't we? Not long now.'

The internal office door slammed, and he hurried to the window of the front room to watch her go. It had been raining and the pavement was slimy, the puddles were black, as though it had rained dirt from above instead of water to clean it away. Jane stood on the kerb, looking around, but not up to wave to him. She stepped aside as a tall man crossed the road towards her. He stared, and leered and said something, but at that moment a taxi came round the corner and Jane hailed it and got in. The scene below, bright as it was with the neon signs reflected on the wet surfaces and the brilliant colours of the fruit and vegetables on the stalls, was immediately darkened for him. That man below was Reg Farrell; what the hell did he think he was doing, staring after Jane like that? What had he said to her?

Reg Farrell was one of Mike's clients. He had been in and out of prison and police cells, always for petty crimes. He had never done anything desperately wicked but that was more for want of ability than for want of trying. He did not doubt that what he did was wrong, and in that, Mike realised, he differed from more successful law-breakers. Reg Farrell thought of himself as a bad 'un, and offered no justification for his various offences. He waged no righteous war with society or capitalism. Perhaps, Mike thought, that was why he, unlike Mike himself, hardly ever got away with it. Unfortunately his uncomplicated attitude to law-breaking had not given him the half-attractive, half-innocent air of some of the people whom Mike defended, who had certainly done what they were accused of. Reg Farrell was an old-fashioned villain, and Mike always regretted that he had not quite the nerve to tell him to find another lawyer.

Reg Farrell disappeared from view, and in a moment Mike heard footsteps coming up to the office door. But he did not go down in answer to the knocks and the rattled handle, and after a while Reg Farrell went away.

The Easter holidays passed all too slowly between sodden mountains and dreary museums. Christine did her best, even Mike could see it. She worked hard at being jokey and cheerful and presenting to Samantha a picture of united and affectionate parents. She used the private language they had made love with once, deferred to his choice of daily outing, and smiled when he and Samantha embraced. On the way back to London in the train she held his hand under the table. Her hand was smooth and hard, with short, very clean nails; they felt less familiar to Mike than his memory of Jane's, which were rough, with picked skin around her long red nails. He rubbed his thumb on Christine's ring, a row of three small diamonds, remembering the prominent sapphire which sparkled on Jane's finger. Jane must have some money; that would help, he thought.

The Ropers got to London the evening before Samantha was to start school, and she was sent to bed early, her room not as yet untidied, her clothes laid out for the morning. Mike and Christine met in her room on the way to bed, she fresh from the bath and smelling of baby powder, he groaning from an evening of opening bills and circulars, and counting the time until Jane would come again.

Christine smiled at her husband and daughter, and said softly, 'Isn't she sweet?' They went together into their bedroom. Christine laid out Mike's clean pyjamas.

'I feel much better for a holiday, don't you, darling?' He grunted, and started to undress.

'There seems to be so little time to see you when we're both working. What with the shopping and cooking and housework, the time goes without us having time to even talk to Samantha, let alone each other.' She took off her dressing-gown and stretched, looking sidelong at her figure in the long glass. 'I've got thinner, don't you think?' He glanced at her and quickly away again, muttering something inaudible. Christine lay on the bed, naked. She stretched her hand out to the box of cigarettes and changed her mind. He had once said, years ago, that smoking in bed turned him off. Mike hastily pulled on his pyjamas, and meaningly knotted the cord.

'Shall we move, Mike? Move house, I mean?' She got up from the bed, and pulled her nightdress from under the pillow, her shoulders set in a dejected slump, but her voice was light. 'I'd rather like to live in the country.'

'I thought you hated the country.' He got under the covers and reached for the *Solicitor's Journal.*

'I wouldn't mind trying. And you'd like it. It would be good for Samantha too. Perhaps we could look up your father's family.'

Mike slammed the magazine on to the floor, and flung himself under the covers. He was damned if he'd talk to Christine about a dream which had a quite different leading lady. He turned off his bedside light while she was in mid-sentence. Why did she have to start talking about that kind of thing now? What had come over her to be so— so conciliating? Couldn't she tell that—? He summoned the image of Jane to his mind, and fell asleep caressing it.

The office had been busy in Mike's absence and his appointments book was full for the next three weeks. There was a longish list of callers who had been referred with problems that wouldn't wait to another firm of solicitors, one of them, he noticed with annoyance, a conveyance of one of the few large houses left in the neighbourhood. The only real money he ever made was on conveyances. The articled clerk explained that the client had been in a hurry to get the contract signed before the purchasers realised that the apparently peaceful meadow at the end of the garden was actually the playing field for a home for disturbed boys who were away for the school holidays. The rest were no loss; two people had said they would call again, one of them Mr Cunningham who was due to move into his high-rise flat next week.

'I think he wants to give you something,' the clerk said. 'A bit of furniture that won't fit in the flat.'

Reg Farrell had called twice too, and said that he would come back when Mr Roper could see him.

As soon as he had a chance Mike took the enamel egg from the back of a filing drawer where he had hidden it. The bulge in his pocket was exactly the size that a hand-grenade would have made, and he was amused to find himself cringing at the sight of policemen. He took the underground train to Kensington High Street, and walked from there slowly up Church Street. It was years since he had been in this district, and he thought the glossy, prosperous appearance of the stucco houses and the elegant shops was odious. The women who bustled past him represented all that he had once thought he hated and he still hated the world they came from, but at least now he could wonder as he looked at them whether they, like Jane, were human underneath.

He would have liked to strip and rape the girl who was serving in the shop he chose to go into, with her long thick hair, her long thin legs, her bold, distant eyes, her expensively casual clothes. She was utterly polite; but he knew that he existed, in her mind, rather less than the poodle which squatted in the gutter.

'We do buy,' she murmured. 'I'm not sure whether—' she flashed him a blank smile. 'Mummy!'

'Coming.' An equally high-pitched reply. Mummy came out from the inner room, a little smaller, slightly less bold, but out of a similar mould. 'Fabergé. Charming. But have you got the rest of it? It would be worth much more if—'

'What do you mean?'

'Well, the thing that was inside. See how something would fit this space? Oh, don't you—? Like those little wooden dolls, you know? Where they nest inside each other?'

'My little girl has one of those. But—'

'That's right. You had one too, Charlotte, do you remember? This egg must have had—I don't know—an animal, would you say?'

'Would it be worth much more complete?'

'Oh lord yes. Worth a packet then. I'm afraid that on its own—perhaps somewhere else.'

'I'll see if I can find them.'

'Yes, *do.*' She smiled broadly, professionally, at him. 'We'd *love* to see it then. That would be marvellous.'

'I'll come back then.'

'Super.'

He thought, 'super'. Ridiculous old bitch. Still, if the egg would be so valuable complete it would be worth going back there; or trying somewhere else. Presumably Jane would be able to bring whatever it was. She can't have realised that the parts were worth less than the whole.

Mike waited impatiently as the days went by. He could hardly bear the sight of his clients, and when he was in court he had to force himself to attend to the words of the other lawyers and the witnesses. He knew what was meant by dry as dust now; as a student he had learnt the law

40

eagerly, relishing the way the information slotted into place. When he was articled he learnt coldly, without involvement. He could not force himself to care what happened to the impersonal companies for whom his principal mostly acted, and when he was dealing with the private clients who employed the firm he felt alienated by their wealth and privileges. It was his work at the law centre which had, in his own words, hit the spot. Suddenly he could see the point of what he had learnt, and told himself that a person with his training would be able to bend and use the system, instead of submitting to it.

It was the picture of himself and Jane living a different life which had soured the practice for him. She bore no relation to the victims he saw all day long. Her charm in the inappropriate surroundings was simply that they were inappropriate; he delighted in the incongruity, and experienced an almost mystic anticipation of the new life which they would lead together, where her proper setting and his would merge.

The first Saturday after getting back from Wales Mike set off by train to East Anglia. He spent a happy day visiting estate agents and riding on the tops of buses around the lanes. He looked at one cottage, but realised that anything suitable was likely to be accessible only by car. It amused him, though, to see as a stranger a cottage probably identical to the one where he had been born. His mother had often described the little flint-faced house, with two bedrooms upstairs and one room downstairs. The one he looked at still had, as his mother had remembered, a black iron stove, with stone slabs on the floor and the plaster bubbling damply off the walls. Even one year ago he would have laughed to scorn the idea that he might ever live in such a place, but now he stood thoughtfully in the old room, his hair brushing against the beams, visualising not the older Roper, swathed in sacks and boots

41

against perpetual rain and mud, but his son, dark suited, with a briefcase, leaving a bright, straw-matted, stripped-pine hideout where a wife who might have been painted by Renoir kissed him goodbye.

He stood in the garden, planning how he too would have parallel rows of vegetables, and bushes studded with berries. I'm a country man at heart, he thought, I've come back to my roots. Just as he was now looking at a thinly sprouting crop (he did not know what it was) so must his ancestors have stood admiring the fruits of their labours. Perhaps, he thought, we'll have a cow. Samantha would grow rosy and strong in the unpolluted air and—his thoughts were interrupted by a flight of jet bombers from an American air force base, and he turned away from the cottage. He and Jane needed something a little larger, a little less uncompromisingly set square to the road. Thatch, he thought, and some trees; perhaps a converted barn, or an oast house, or even a windmill.

The next day it rained, and Mike sat in his upstairs flat, watching the greyness of London streets and recalling the verdant countryside he had seen the day before. Christine read the papers industriously. He thought how she would look out of place in his new home, and how Jane would fit into the country setting. Samantha, he thought, would like to have a dog. Christine began to speak once or twice, but checked herself. She and Samantha played Scrabble and draughts, talking in low voices. Christine said Samantha should not make a noise; couldn't she see her father was thinking?

There was no letter from Jane at the office on Monday to say that she would come this week but Mike did not take any notice of that, for the post, as everyone in London knew, was very erratic. He would send the staff off early on the half day and lay in some special delicacies. Mr Cunningham turned up with a huge marble clock, which the old man could hardly carry. He and his wife wanted it to go to a good home, he explained. Mike put it on the mantelpiece of his office, wondering whether the shelf would stand the strain. There were no mantelpieces in the new flats, it seemed, but the new cooker the council had provided had an electric clock on it.

Mike went out in the lunch hour to get some food. He went to the large store down the road, and while he was there chose a new shirt, for which he paid, and some socks, which he 'liberated'. He hesitated in the food section; eggs, wine, fruit. He knocked a jar of peaches in brandy and a polythene packet of smoked salmon into his carrier bag. There was a queue at the checkout desk, and Mike read a magazine about housekeeping while he waited, slotting it back into the stand when it came to his turn to pay. He walked along the aisle to the front doors, looking at the pristine women's underclothes and a stand of improbable hats and wondering why he found it so hard to imagine Jane in any of them. She probably even wore hats, in her old life.

He looked up to see Reg Farrell looking both dirty and shifty, fingering men's jerseys with ash dripping from his cigarette on to the wool.

'Hullo then, Mr Roper,' he said in a whining voice. 'I been waiting to see you.'

'Hullo Reg,' Mike said unenthusiastically. 'You in trouble again?'

'Oh no sir, no indeed. Nothing like that. No, that's a thing of the past, you might say.'

'Well, I'm glad to hear it.'

'No, like I say, I've learnt me lesson. Not a very nice thing to do, lifting things. I realise that now. I mean to say, how'd you like it then, having your things nicked?'

'What do you want then? Get on with it, Reg, do. I haven't got all day.'

43

'Now then, now then, Mr Roper, that ain't a nice way to talk at all. I don't take kindly to that, I don't. My money's as good as anyone else's, I hope. Innit?'

'I expect so.' Mike edged to one side. 'I'll see you in the office, Reg. Make an appointment.'

'Not so fast, Mr Roper, if you don't mind.'

'I do mind. I've got a lot to do.'

'Your lady friend coming, is she?'

'What the hell are you talking about?'

'Got something nice for her today? Giving her a bit of a treat?'

Mike gaped at the man; Reg put out his hand and with surprising firmness took hold of Mike's carrier bag. 'Wouldn't do you no good with that lawyers' society, or whatever you call it, would it? Wouldn't look good in the daily paper. Now if I was to call one of the shop detectives, wouldn't they have a surprise? Who'd have thought it, a respectable pillar of the bloody community, no less. Make a change from having me in the dock, I'll say that.'

'Lower your voice, man,' Mike said angrily.

'Not quite the article for anyone to hear, is it? I can see that.'

'What do you want?' Mike muttered. He had not, somehow, ever thought of bracketing himself with a man like Farrell; his own habits were established on so different a philosophical foundation from the savage and mindless behaviour of his recidivist clients that he had never thought to compare them; which was odd now he came to think of it. He started to shoplift years before, as an articled clerk, making his own private, conscious protest against the world of privilege with which he was forced to be concerned. It was perhaps the most notable gesture he could have made, for his own appreciation alone; he had been taught not to steal as was any conventional mother's son; but the prohibition was reinforced because the children who were

44

thieves stole from his own family. The sort of shop Mike's mother kept was always the target for petty pilferers, who became, in the Roper family's demonology, a very direct enemy. So his improbably criminal behaviour had been at first an expression of Mike's own personality. Self-justification, invented at a later stage, listed all the arguments about capitalism and greed which Mike had by then heard. But it was a long time since he had worried about the rationale behind his actions. He slipped stolen goods in a bag or a pocket as casually as if he were entitled to do so. Reg Farrell's words shocked him, of course, and he felt a flush of blood running up his forehead, and cold and chilly down his spine, but his horror was caused as much by surprise at having his actions questioned as by fear.

'You think you're different than the likes of me, don't you?' Farrell said, in an unconscious echo of Mike's thoughts. 'All right for you to knock off what you want for your fancy woman, innit? All the time yer being so high and mighty and big professional man. You behave as though you had a right to it.'

'What do you want?' Mike repeated.

'Cash.'

'We can't talk here. Come to the office.'

'Not likely.' The man sneered, and moved to stand more directly in front of Mike. He looked round to see whether they were attracting notice, but the shop was not full, and being as usual short-staffed, the nearest assistant was twenty yards away beside her cash register. The very fact that the staff did not supervise the customers more closely was, of course, what had made Mike's stealing so simple, as it had made so many of his less competent clients think it would be. It was a measure of how he had grown to take his own behaviour for granted that he never even made comparisons between it and that of his

45

accused clients, when he was with them in court on shop-lifting charges.

'I'm not letting you out of here with that bagful,' Farrell went on. 'So long as you're this side of these doors you're red-handed, aren't you? Nah, no use trying to put the bag down. They remember who bought that lot. You're known round here, ain't you?'

'So what are you going to do about it?'

'Nothing if you pay. It's as simple as that.'

'How do you mean?'

'Oh, come on. Don't act daft.'

'I haven't any money on me.'

'I believe you. A cheque will do, thanks. Got your cheque book? And don't go thinking you'll have time to stop it. It would take a lot of explaining. After all, why'd you write a cheque out to me, people would want to know? Make it enough and I'll keep quiet about your lady friend too.'

'I don't care if you tell it from Hyde Park Corner about her.'

'Oh, that's nice, good. So you wouldn't mind if her hubby knew your name and address then? I'll remember that.' Mike stared at the man, his mind temporarily paralysed. 'Got yer cheque book, have yer?'

'I suppose so.'

'That's right. Make it out to Reginald Farrell, Esquire. Seven hundred and fifty pounds, shall we say? Makes a nice compromise between five hundred and a thousand.'

'You're mad. I haven't got seventy-five,' Mike said, in an urgent whisper. He was suddenly terrified that someone might notice him talking to the disreputable-looking man and wonder why he was writing him a cheque. For write him a cheque he certainly must. Outside those swinging glass doors he would be safe, his bagful as apparently his own by law as the clothes on his back. But trapped inside the shop by the malodorous figure of Reg Farrell he was in jeopardy. If he paid him a bit now, and got outside, that would be it. The blackmail couldn't be repeated, for he would never put himself in a position again where the man could prove that Mike had committed a crime. He would enjoy thinking up a suitable retribution for the blackmailer, probably in the form of information laid with the police which would lead to prosecution and imprisonment. Yes, Reg Farrell would be sorry he had tried his tricks out on a canny lawyer, Mike promised himself.

'Seven hundred and fifty, or I'll call the fuzz.'

'It would only bounce,' Mike said.

'Yeah? Can't you get nothing from your rich friend then? That mink she wears didn't cost fifty pee, you know. Oh, you've got funds to draw on, don't you worry. I shouldn't let it bounce if I was you, mate. Here's my pen. Nicked from the post office, treat it carefully. Seven hundred and fifty smackers on the line, if you please.'

Mike was trapped. He wanted to bang his fists on the counter behind him, scatter the pile of multicoloured garments about, scream and tear his hair. He half turned to put the cheque book on to the glass shelf, and wrote out the cheque Farrell had demanded. 'There you are, damn your eyes. But you won't be able to draw the money.'

'I'd make sure I can, if I was you, Mr Roper.' He folded the paper and put it into an inside pocket. His jacket was stained with grease and its lining was torn. It would have been disagreeable to touch. He moved his foot from the carrier bag. 'Here you are, your shopping. Have a nice meal with your lady friend.'

It should have been easy enough for Mike to get hold of Jane. Even once he had realised that she would need to be traced by investigation, because she could not be looked up in a telephone book, he would have thought that his almost unique experience of tracing missing persons for his clients would have made it simple for him to track Jane down. In a practice with a middle-class clientele, tracing missing persons is unusual. It is hard for someone oppressed by mortgages, insurances, old school acquaintances, bank accounts and other such incubi, to drop out completely. In Mike's world the apparently permanent disappearance was much more frequent. He was well experienced in the technique of detection and advertisement, the 'when did you last see your father' and the 'do you recognise this photograph' questions, the lists in Sunday papers, the Salvation Army's limitless awareness. But he could hardly use the systems he had so often tried for his clients when it came to finding Jane Shore; if for no other reason, because he had no photograph—indeed, no paper details about her at all. He could describe her appearance, and knew her name; but no more.

Mike could hardly believe that Jane was not going to come back. He waited for her evening after evening, and as each early-closing day came he was certain that she would appear; he stood cramped at the window, watching for taxis to turn the corner and desolated when they did not stop. He stood so long that his legs grew stiff and his throat smoke dry. The air of early summer, even in this slum, mocked him with a promise of happiness. Mike lusted to see Jane. He felt like someone with an inaccessible itching, irritable and wretched.

There was another reason, as well as his own desire, which made Mike desperate for Jane to come to him again. Reg Farrell had cashed the cheque which Mike had written. Mike had been forced to draw on his clients' account to meet it. And in the autumn, when the auditors came, he would be discovered, accused and struck off. Yet £750 was a small sum; the sum represented a peccadillo, not a peculation, he assured himself. It would be met, easily, by the sale of, for instance, Jane's mink coat; or the Fabergé egg, no doubt, would bring in more than that, if only he had the chance to tell Jane to bring the other bits of it.

Mike wondered whether her husband was keeping her prisoner, for surely she would come if she could. Even if her children were ill, he thought, or if she were ill herself, she would at least have let him know. If only he could get in touch with her. But he did not have any idea where she lived. He did not know her husband's first name, her maiden name, her age, her place of birth, even the names of her children. He might have imagined her very existence, and by the end of his hours of vigil he would say to himself, 'Sister Anne, Sister Anne, you won't see anyone coming. She was only a figment of imagination in the first place.'

At the end of May Mike realised that it was no use waiting any longer. Jane was his only hope for raising the money; he could no more raise £750 himself than fly. Christine, who was being so tactful and forbearing that he would happily have wrung her neck, had nothing. Every penny she earned went to pay their rent. There was no means of finding the money through his practice that he could think of; the most he could hope to make from his next volume of law cases for children was two hundred pounds, of which his agent would take twenty, and which the publishers would not advance without having the manuscript. He decided to go and see the people at Palfrey & Blackwood.

John Blackwood was polite, but showed that he was amused, for Mike allowed him to think that he had been remembering a vision of Jane Shore since the Palfrey & Blackwood party the previous autumn.

'I don't actually deal with her work myself,' he said. 'It's a little—' he gestured elegantly, to indicate that feminine porn was beneath him. 'But I'll find out.' He made various telephone calls to women called Atalanta, Melissa and Rowena. Finally a girl whom he introduced as Guinevere came into his room with a sheet of paper from which he read aloud, ' "Ms Jane Shore, 17 Belgrave Street".'

'Is that her home address?'

'Is it, Guinevere?'

'Actually, Johnny, no. I think that Davie did ask her, but she said she'd always get things sent on.'

'Well, I think we should have our authors' addresses,' John Blackwood complained. 'Get Davie to ask her again, will you, Guinevere? I suppose Jane Shore is her name, is it?'

'Well, actually, Johnny,' she began, seeming, Mike thought, more nervous than an editorial assistant should be in a firm which was so committed to nicknamed matiness between the owner's son and the junior employees, 'actually I'm not sure that it is. I'm awfully sorry. Davie did tell her that she had to—but you know how it is— if people just don't answer questions in letters—she never comes to the office ...'

'She was here at the party.'

'Yes, well, it wasn't really the place to pin her down.'

'She should never have been paid until—'

'Well but Johnny—'

'Oh, all right, Guinevere. It's not your fault. Take Mike here along to Romance and give him a copy of her ghastly epic.'

Guinevere led Mike along dark corridors and down narrow staircases to Romance's dungeon.

'I really am sorry, Mr Roper,' she said. 'It's awfully embarrassing. I don't know what Johnny will say when you aren't there to hear. But Jane Shore simply wouldn't— well, you can see why, if you read the book. It's not the sort of thing you'd want the neighbours to know you'd written. I didn't think we'd ever see her, actually. She had written to say she didn't think she'd be able to come to that party. Davie said she was probably a famous don at Oxford, or a judge or something—you know, a person who'd be really dished if it got out that she was writing a book like *A Pleasure to Come*. We did ask her for a publicity photo, but she wouldn't send one.'

'It's hot stuff, isn't it?' Mike said, admiring Guinevere's figure as she walked in front of him.

'It is rather. It seems hotter because a woman wrote it, if you know what I mean.'

Mike did know what she meant. In fact he found that there was something suggestive and sexy about even mentioning the book, whose torrid passages he vividly recalled, to another woman, but Guinevere was as detached as a doctor about her work and glanced unblushing and apparently unmoved through the copy of it which she took from the shelf in her room.

'I think it's a one-off, actually,' she said. She handed the volume to him, and he put it between the letters in a dull file, in his briefcase. 'My guess is that she said her all, in that. You know, the autobiographical first novel, plus some wish-fulfilment. I'd guess that Jane Shore has a dull

51

life in the country with a dull and worthy husband and dreams about sheikhs and fur hearthrugs and ineffable romance while she peels the potatoes. For what it's worth.'

Belgravia was off Mike's beat, and he had some trouble in finding the right street; once there, he had more difficulty in identifying number 17. It turned out to be a secret-looking house, with two brass plates let into the stone beside a black door. One had the name of a well-known chain of betting shops; the other said 'The Country Club, Second Floor'.

At the back of Mike's mind lurked an image of clubs which included Corinthian pillars and fatherly hall porters. Here he went up carpeted stairs to a pink front door, which opened on to a small lobby furnished with a pink carpet and some chintz and a desk which looked very much like a kidney-shaped dressing-table, draped with muslin. The bell was answered by a rigidly corseted woman who wore a kind of apricot-coloured paste on her ageing face.

'I'm trying to get hold of Jane Shore.'

'Oh yes.'

'I think she may be one of your members.'

'Do you?'

'Well, can you tell me how to—?'

'I am afraid we preserve strict confidentiality about our membership.'

'Well, how can I—?'

'You could leave a letter for her.'

'Are you expecting her to come and collect her mail? I used to know her when I was young,' he added, suddenly inspired. 'We lived next door. I've been abroad for the last few years, and her family has moved away. Nobody seems to know—I do so want to see her again. I'd be so very much obliged if you—' He bent his most practised bird-charming smile on her. The woman's mask-like face cracked into wrinkles, and she smiled at him almost indulgently.

'Young love,' she said. 'How it all comes back. I'll see what I can do.' She went into a small office, leaving the door open, and Mike could see her hunting through drawers. He sat down on a velvet-coated toadstool, and tried to count the number of roses in one square yard of the chintz curtain. The air felt heavy and dead. There was no sound of traffic, but women's voices could be heard from somewhere in the house. Two haughty women with ten-gallon hats and fur coats went past him without a glance. Mike lit a cigarette, and flicked the match into a bowl of plastic roses which stood on a mahogany flower-stand. In the steel fireplace were arranged purple and brown dried flowers. He wondered what would happen if he put a match to a corner of one of the leaves. It was curious how the smell was not of scent, but of scented things, perhaps powder, or deodorant. He felt unable to imagine Jane here.

The woman came back holding an index card. 'It's funny,' she said. 'Mrs Shore's been a member here for several months now, but she hasn't actually taken a room. Most of our ladies—' The front door opened at this moment, and a vivacious blonde woman, wearing a vermilion suit, went through into the rest of the apartment, followed by a man in navy pin-stripes who had an inordinately furtive air. The woman to whom Mike had been speaking did not glance at them, but fixed her eyes on the index card, and only lifted her gaze to Mike's face when the baize door had stopped swinging.

'Wasn't that—?' Mike began.

'No names here, please,' the woman interrupted. Mike thought, I don't believe it. He said,

'Did you say that Mrs Shore hasn't stayed here?'

'I haven't a record of any room numbers on her card, no,' she said. 'As a matter of fact I can't put a face to her at all. I've forwarded quite a few letters, of course.'

'Where do you send them?'

'I'm not sure that I can—'

'Please,' he urged. 'I really am longing to get in touch with her.'

'How did you get this address in the first place?' she said. 'If she didn't tell you herself—I can't understand how—'

'I've been hunting for Jane,' he said, passionately, 'all over London. I've asked everyone. At last I was told— I won't say his name—a very important person said that he always knew Jane would get his letters if he addressed them here. So I came.'

'Well, I don't suppose I'd be giving away much if I tell you that her mail gets sent on to the Royal Counties Bank. The Piccadilly branch. But then, they mostly cover their tracks,' she added, with a sudden gleam of malice; and immediately covered her mouth with her hand, staring at him with worried, monkey eyes. 'Don't say I told you.'

Mike passed another couple on the stairs; the man had a face he should have been able to put a name to. Mike paused on the pavement outside and looked up at the windows which must be those of the Country Club, the top two floors of the house; all shrouded with net curtains, as he would have expected. He imagined the rooms behind. Would they just provide beds, he wondered, luxurious as they might be, or would refinements be available? He dredged his memory for reports of such establishments in the newspapers. There might, he supposed, be two-way mirrors, perhaps a gymnasium. Once he had found Jane again, he would make damned sure that they progressed from his dusty divan to the lusher pastures of the Country Club.

But fancy, Jane! he thought repeatedly. It took, he felt, a lot of swallowing, to believe that Jane knew that her accommodation address was that of a brothel; or, he amended, not quite that. He would call it a house of ill

54

fame. Pleased with this old-fashioned description, he turned towards a pub.

The bank, he knew, would be an uncrackable nut. There was no point in any direct attempt to get them to divulge Jane's home address. On the other hand, he could hardly believe that even hₑr mania for covering her tracks could have taken a further step. The Royal Counties Bank was bound to know, even if they would not tell, where she lived.

Somehow the discovery that Jane's elusiveness had been created by her, rather cleverly too, changed Mike's feelings about his search. When it had been possible to suppose that she had been merely absent-minded, or even secretive, when he had been certain that the most simple questions would elicit the answer he needed, he had felt hesitant about making those few necessary enquiries. Now it was clear that the image he had in his mind of Jane Shore was inaccurate. If he had not loved her, he would have said that she deserved what was coming to her.

Mike had frequently employed Challis Peters, Private Enquiry Agents, on behalf of his clients, and had long since got over his surprise at finding that the Challis half of the partnership was a motherly looking woman, by now about fifty years old. She had worked for years in an Employment Exchange, and had taken the unusual step of leaving it to set up in partnership with a man who had been one of her most persistent customers. He simply didn't like doing what other people told him to do, Alan Peters had explained, but when you were job hunting it was difficult to insist on being your own boss. Miss Challis liked him, and sympathised, and their friendship, uneasily born across an official desk, developed into a trusting relationship; by now, fifteen years after they had first met, they worked together in perfect harmony. Their clients were undistinguished and their own work undramatic. It was quite unlike the fictional idea of a private detective's job. Indeed, they very rarely tried to trace anyone who particularly wanted not to be found, for their subjects had usually disappeared as a result of laziness about letter writing rather than malice aforethought.

'Banks are difficult, you know, Mike,' Miss Challis said thoughtfully. 'Is that the only line we've got?'

'It's the only one my clients could give me,' he said, having, for the first time that he could remember, not told Miss Challis the truth.

'I'm not sure that it's quite our—well, perhaps another firm?'

'My dear Dot. I haven't used another firm since I set up on my own. You don't mean it.'

'You'll have to talk to Alan about it,' she said. Mike knew that he was home and dry, as he put it in his mind. But he was mistaken. Dorothy Challis dropped in on him after work a week later. He was still in the office, for although part of his mind had taken to thinking of Jane as an opponent, to be caught by any available means, another part still believed that she would return to him as before. Every day he felt hope blossoming as the time came for his staff to leave.

Dorothy Challis dropped into his client's chair and pushed her sensible shoes off her feet. 'I'm whacked. I've been chasing after a runaway kid all day. Walked out from home, and the police don't care as she's seventeen. She was supposed to take A Levels and go to University this year. Anyway, your enquiry about Jane Shore.'

'Yes?' he asked eagerly.

'It's no go, I'm afraid.'

'What?'

'We can't get any further. I'm sorry, Mike. 1 didn't realise that you took this one personally.'

'But Dot, there must be some way—'

'Not unless you've got some other info. Alan got hold of

one of the girls working in the Royal Counties Bank. Theatre, night club, you know. Hope your client can afford it. She looked it up, and said the only address was in Belgrave Street. Well, that's a club so-called. Provides bedrooms for rich girls to take their boyfriends. I'd heard of it. And the only address they had—'

'I know, the Bank.' Mike was riven with disappointment. 'But the Bank must have more details. A reference—anything.'

'Apparently she gave a publisher as a reference, when she started the account. Only last year, it was. She paid in two hundred and fifty pounds in cheque form from Palfrey & Blackwood. And I gather from you that they couldn't help either. I could try them if you thought—'

'No, I'm sure they don't know. But that takes us round in a circle.'

'You've tried Somerset House, of course?'

'No, though I suppose I must. Do you think there's much point? After all, it doesn't seem very likely that Jane Shore is her real name!' he said despondently. The sensation of having been betrayed threatened to overwhelm him, and he put his head in his hands and closed his eyes.

'Tell me what you know about her. Everything.' Dot Challis took off her coat, and sat back. 'I have some time. Perhaps I can help.'

'It's good of you.' He thought, I can't tell her much. 'All that I know is that she is married, has two children, lives in the country and probably isn't called Jane Shore. I could do an identikit picture.'

'Where in the country, didn't she say?'

'No, though it's presumably within daily reach of London. I don't even know which station she travelled from.'

'Did she never mention her background, where she went to school, anything like that?'

'No, except that it was in London. And they went in

57

crocodiles round the National Gallery. Actually, her husband must be a farmer, now I come to think of it. She said something about seeing how crops were coming along ...'

'What sort of book did she write?'

'Oh, very sexy. Not much story to it. The girl at the publisher said it was an autobiographical novel. It's what you might call extremely frank. I don't think you'd like it, Dot.'

'That doesn't tell us much either', but as Dorothy Challis ruminated Mike thought that perhaps it did tell them something. If the book was autobiographical, presumably some of the details would match those in Jane's life. The difficulty would be to find out which of them did. But as far as he remembered the heroine was married to a country squire. Dorothy left, promising to think and come back, and Mike settled down at his desk, with paper for making notes, with his copy of a *A Pleasure to Come*.

But it was difficult to extract much that was useful for his purpose from the uninhibited adventures of Lady Babs Gwynne. The descriptions of her life in public were brief, and concentrated on events like her arrival at balls, sweeping up marble staircases, or her swimming naked in clear waters, with the footman to whom she had made passionate love earlier in the day bringing her iced drinks with undiminished formality.

Mike lustfully read again some passages which he already knew almost by heart, and as he read he could recreate the image of Jane, her scent in his nostrils, her softness in his arms. 'Babs rode astride the sailor,' he read, 'and all his strength flowed into her in a shower of brilliant stars, a blaze of Christmas tree lights, he was there for more, he pinned her down tearing her body from her brain ...'

Rubbish, Mike thought, moving uneasily on his chair as desire trickled through him. He turned some pages. 'Babs dived to probe in the deepest darkest places. Her tongue ran through the narrow aisle and he thickened and throbbed ...' Mike slammed the book shut. It made him want her too much, but told him nothing. That last scene, when the sailor and Lady Babs, both naked, chased each other around the floors of a Chinese pagoda, climaxing with what sounded like sex on a flying trapeze, was much padded with descriptions of the interior of, and the view from, the pagoda: a red spire set in green woods and fields. Such autobiography as there might be was too well camouflaged in invention to be distinguishable.

Throughout these days Mike had been living his normal life, seeing clients, appearing for them in court, drafting briefs to counsel, dictating letters. His attention had never been so concentrated on his work for its diversion to be especially noticeable. The people he employed had never been individuals to him, except a few of the prettier girls, and then it had not been what they said that he noticed. If his articled clerk was ill it affected him rather as it affected Christine when her washing machine was broken, with irritation, not concern. That the boy should choose this moment to come down with glandular fever seemed proof of Mike's suspicion that a hostile fate was out to get him. The temptation to abandon his office was ever present: after all, if he failed to get hold of some money to make good the deficit in his clients' account before the autumn, he would have no choice in the matter. Meanwhile he plodded on with the dusty chores. His behaviour at home had become automatic. He could sit at the office desk and if he had been asked would have answered that Christine had certainly served his breakfast that morning, that Samantha chattered to him as he ate it, that the newspaper-seller told him it was a fine day, but the events had left no impression on his memory. It was weeks since he had actually looked at his wife. But habit took him only so far; he felt such a frenzy of impatience and irritation now as he listened to his wretched clients, such paroxysms of restlessness in court, as he could hardly hide.

He dealt abruptly with a group of young people who were squatting in a derelict house near the railway arch. The sight of their brilliantly patterned clothes, and an innocence of expression which a longer acquaintanceship with the minutiae of the Rent Acts would surely change, affected him disagreeably. He shoved his scrawled note of their complaint into the folder and pushed it to the back of the desk. Linda came in with the papers he would need in court.

'You'd better go down, Mr Roper,' she said. 'The clerk rang up, they'll reach you this afternoon.'

'I should have briefed counsel,' he groaned. She pulled his gown and some grubby bands from the cupboard. She was a capable-looking young woman with an irritating air of knowing better than he did. She had told him she wanted to do something useful while she earned her living, and felt that a secretary in his sort of practice would have a chance of that.

'The District Nurse rang up. There's a Mrs Evans wants to make her will. It'll have to be today.'

'I can't. Not today.'

'I said you could go after court. She's dying, Mr Roper.'

'Why me? There's other solicitors.'

'It seems she's been to you before. I've put some will forms in your case.'

His client met him at the door of the court, a bewildered Jamaican with her hostile son of fifteen who was up for theft of a motor bike.

Mike sat on the bench outside, waiting for the case to be called. He counted the repeat of the patterned tiles on the floor.

'Well, it's Mr Roper again.' Reg Farrell was standing beside him, in the company of another solicitor. 'Long time no see. I go to Mr Kahn now.'

'Poor Mr Kahn,' Mike muttered. He knew Philip Kahn from many other cases. He was young and still an idealist, and worked at the law centre at which Mike had once been employed. He treated Mike as a novice monk might treat a man who had abandoned holy orders, and when he was in a good mood Mike was amused, and wondered how long it would take him to realise what the world was really like. Reg Farrell sat down beside Mike, ignoring the two Jamaicans, who stared glumly at him. An usher walked by, and said sharply to the boy, 'No smoking here.'

'Ain't seen your lady friend for a while,' Farrell said. Philip Kahn bustled into the court room, and Farrell winked after him. 'He's on the ball, all right. Get me off I shouldn't wonder. It's only drunk and disorderly this time.' Mike got up and said to his clients, 'We'll go in, shall we?'

They shuffled ahead of him towards the swing doors. Mike was struck by a sudden thought. He said, 'Farrell, did you ever follow my friend?'

'Why d'yer ask?'

'Mind your own business.'

'No, don't worry. I never saw where she went. Scared of her old man, are you? I wouldn't tell on you, Mr Roper, you know me better than that. Never got farther than the ticket office with her, I didn't.'

'The ticket office?'

'Yeah, at Waterloo. "Single to Halemouth", ever so lady-like.' His high-pitched mimic of Jane's accent collapsed into a sneer. 'Didn't think you'd ever let on where she was going, did I?'

'No, Reg, you didn't,' Mike said, dazed. He went into the court room, and sat down in a shaft of dusty red sunlight; the fumed oak was matched by the equivalent stained glass. Halemouth: was that Hampshire, or Dorset? Somewhere on the south coast. What a stroke of luck, he thought, and having heard the magistrate deal quickly with his own

61

client, though he hardly noticed what the verdict was, he stayed where he was to listen to Reg Farrell being sent down for nine months.

He was half way back to the office when he remembered about Mrs Evans's will. He hated visiting clients in their own premises. He was only summoned when they could not get out and usually when they were in extremis; they would be in stuffy, smelly beds and their frailty reproached him. He had never liked being in the same room as some-one who was sick.

Mrs Evans lived in an area of re-development, in one of a pair of brick cottages, loomed over now by a tower of flats with a launderette and a shabby supermarket on the ground floor. What had once been a narrow residential street had become one of the routes through which heavy traffic was directed. In the front garden, which consisted of a square yard of dirt, with a path short enough to have been made of one flagstone, half-a-dozen purple irises stood amongst rusty cans and empty bottles. The windows were hung with curtains, the pattern of wild flowers facing outwards, and the front step had been brushed, not all that long ago, with red lead. A tabby cat brushed against Mike's ankles as he stood at the door, and came in with him when a woman opened it. She seemed to know Mike and jerked her thumb towards the stairs.

'She's in bed, Mr Roper. Nurse said she'd be back later. I'll just nip out a minute.'

The house smelt of lavender, and pungent furniture polish. The stairs had a worn turkey carpet on them, and thickly encrusted paper running up the sides. Every time a lorry went along the road outside the walls seemed to shake. Mike mounted into a sick-room, bathroom, smell. Mrs Evans was in the back bedroom, which was almost filled by a high mahogany bedstead, on which voluminous quilts and pillows were folded. The old woman was sitting in a high-backed chair by the window. She looked quite alert and spry, and her aged hands twitched a pink shawl more closely around her as Mike came into the room. Her voice was very high, and toneless, but firm, with an educated accent.

'It's good of you to come,' she said. 'I didn't mean to leave it to the last moment like this—making my will, I mean.'

'I'm sure it isn't really—' he said automatically.

'Oh, don't be embarrassed. We all have to go sometime.'

'I didn't mean that, Mrs Evans. But you did make a will, not so long ago, after your daughter died. You left it all to your nephew.'

'My daughter isn't dead! What can you be thinking of! She went away, that's all.' She paused, breathing heavily, and leant forward to drink something through a straw that was propped up in a glass on her side table. Mike put his case down, and looked out of the window. The view was on to a railway line. The signal was just below. There was no television set in the room, but a large, ancient wireless stood on the table, and there were piles of tatty books stacked up against the walls. Mrs Evans saw him glancing at them.

'My landlady is so good to me,' she said. 'Most women would mind that sort of mess. Not to speak of wanting to turn me out to the workhouse when I got ill.'

She sat back with her eyes closed, and Mike picked up one of the books so as not to seem impatient. It was what he believed was called a coffee-table volume, about gardens and their ornaments, borrowed from the Public Library. He glanced unmoved at photographs of tumbling pink roses, wisteria-draped conservatories, and box hedges trimmed in the shape of chessmen. He was putting the book down when it fell open at a picture which drew his attention; a symmetrical view of a building, framed by tall dark trees, with blue sky and bluer water behind it. The building was a lacquer-red pagoda.

'Write it down,' the old woman whispered. 'I want to sign it at once, as soon as the nurse gets here. For my darling Eirlys.' Mike rested a will form on the book and wrote rapidly. He looked up when he had finished, and saw that Mrs Evans had fallen asleep, her toffee-coloured eyes closed again. The front door slammed, and brisk footsteps sounded on the stairs.

'Oh, you got here, did you?' The District Nurse came in. There was hardly room for two people to stand in the room.

'She wants me to make a will in favour of her daughter who died last year,' he whispered.

'I'd better speak to her.'

'She hasn't anything to leave,' he said. 'I guess it's just as easy to go along with her.' The nurse stepped forward.

'Mrs Evans, dear, let's be seeing you,' she said heartily. Then she leant a little closer, and picked up the wrinkled wrist. 'You might as well be on your way, Mr Roper,' she said without turning round. He heard the rattle of the curtain rings when he was half down the stairs. He was still holding the book about gardens, and stuffed it into his case, before stepping out into the street.

PART TWO

Hugh passed by the open door of the drawing-room when he came in from the evening check of the animals, and he frowned slightly as his eye fell on the girl; he leant in to pull the door closed before he went to pour himself a drink in the pantry.

Lindsay did not look up, but she had noticed him, and thought she knew what he was thinking: that she did not enhance her surroundings. Lindsay sat with her feet pulled up on the sofa. Her toenails scratched against the threads in the flowery loose cover. She was wearing an Indian cotton skirt in colours which clashed with the muted chintzes and velvets. Her feet were cold, and she covered them with a cushion embroidered in gros-point needlework. She thrust her hand through her long thick hair and scratched flecks of dandruff from her scalp, and then she vigorously shook her head. The room was delicately fragrant, of potpourri and nicotiana, strategically planted below the window so that its night scent would be appreciated. There were magazines on the footstool, books in the shelf-filled alcoves, new novels from the subscription library on the sofa table. Hugh had turned on the television in the sitting-room. Behind the door a stack of records waited to entertain her. Nobody could say, Lindsay thought, that anything was wanting in this house. She picked at a corn on her little toe, sliding a finger nail under a loose flap of skin and relishing the slight twinge of pain. Then she got up and walked over to the window. The carpet was thin under her bare feet, she could feel the lines of the floor boards under it. There was a parquet surround and as she stood by the long window she moved her foot to and fro across its waxy smoothness. The garden was dark, and the trees were silhouettes against a greenish sky. The night was perfectly calm. In her romantic adolescence Lindsay had been unspeakably moved by rural stillness. One night she had run out on to the lawn, barefoot in a demure nightdress, her feet not hardened by habit then, but the grass as comfortable to them as velvet, and she had danced with what felt like heartfelt grace. She remembered the episode as one of pure emotion, performed to no seeing eye.

Lindsay opened the glass doors and stepped across the terrace, and down the three steps on to the lawn. It was damp, and fragments of cut grass stuck to her feet. She felt no joy: only a slight discomfort.

The sound of a car approached along the drive. Lindsay went into the drawing-room. She left grassy footmarks on the pale carpet, but took no notice of them. She could hear her sister coming in through the back door, and slamming and bolting it behind her. Her footsteps tapped along the stone flags into the sitting-room, and Hugh and she spoke briefly; then she came along to the drawing-room.

'Hullo, everything all right?' Venetia said predictably. She went to the windows and drew the three pairs of curtains across them, and then she moved towards the fireplace and started to make tidy stacks of the magazines, and to fold up *The Times*.

'Did you have much to do?' Lindsay asked.

'Much—what do you mean?'

'The dentist—'

'Oh, yes. All done now.'

'It's a long course of treatment.'

'Yes, well, I'd left it for a long time. What have you been doing all day?'

'Damn all.'

'Oh dear—you make it sound so boring.'

'Doesn't do me any harm.'

'Were the children good?' Venetia asked, but she did not seem to notice that Lindsay could not be bothered to answer. Weren't the children always good, after all? And if by any chance they had misbehaved, was she likely to get them into trouble by saying so? Lindsay could well remember sharing Venetia's sulks in the linen cupboard when their mother made the very sort of crass remarks which Venetia now perpetrated. Venetia sat on the other sofa, and rested her head against its back, her eyes closed. Black, Lindsay thought, did not suit her.

'You look very tired,' she said.

'Knackered, as Henry would say. The train was late.'

'Shall I get you a drink?' Lindsay asked. Venetia pushed herself up from the chair, taking her weight on her wrists like an old woman.

'You're the one that's supposed to be resting.'

'Nonsense, let me—'

In the end they went into the kitchen together. 'It's silly, Venetia, why can't you let me wait on you for a change? Look, go to bed, I'll bring you a tray.'

'I shouldn't dream of it. Look, I'll make you a hottie while I've got the kettle on.' She poured the water into the bottle with pursed-mouth concentration, and then stood with her bottom against the Aga's towel rail, hugging the hot rubber to her stomach. 'Let the tea stew for a minute.'

'What else did you do in London?' Lindsay asked.

'Nothing really. Walked miles—you know how one does.' As though reminded of her feet, she kicked off her high-heeled shoes.

'I don't actually. Take taxis everywhere.'

'Oh well, you live there.'

'I've been here so long I've almost forgotten that I do.'

'We love having you.'

'I don't think Hugh does,' Lindsay said. When she used, as a child, to stay with her glamorously married sister, Hugh had treated her in an affectionate and brotherly way. But he had never swung himself into the modern world. He did not now like her clothes or hair and he positively deplored her lifestyle. He was polite and disapproving, where he had once been teasing and affectionate.

'Perhaps he's afraid of my influence on Harriet.'

'I shouldn't think he is,' Venetia said, yawning.

'He thinks I'll unsettle her. Give her ideas about being something other than a good wife and mother.'

'He won't mind what she does, as long as she's happy.'

'Pious talk. You know how he deplores the life I lead.'

'Lindsay, I'm simply too tired.' Venetia handed the hot-water bottle to her sister, and walked across the wide kitchen to check that the sink taps were turned off tightly and the door locked. 'I can only sleep easy behind bars,' she said. 'Hugh thinks it's silly. They never locked the doors at all when he was little.'

'It's the London childhood,' Lindsay agreed. 'Made us suspicious.'

The kitchen had red tiles on the floor, a huge wooden table, and red and white paint. The Aga hissed gently and the red formica tops were bare. It was not a room for tidiness, for the late evening. In the morning, Venetia would come down early, put the frozen rolls in the hot oven, feed the cats, water the geranium, fill the room with the smells of bacon and coffee. Lindsay did not like to see it with the traces of her own dutiful hand on it. All day she had felt that Hugh and the children were made uneasy by her alien presence in Venetia's territory, by her impatience with the extra details of comfort which she could

68

never be bothered to add to the essential nourishment. Napkins which the children would not unroll, side plates off which nobody ate bread, flowers in the table centre which everyone ignored—these were the little things which occupied Venetia. Yet it was pleasant when she was there to provide them.

Lindsay went thankfully into the spare bedroom which had been hers for the last few months. She would never have chosen to paint a room in shades of pink, or to cover the bed and chairs in a flowery chintz to match the curtains, yet it was comfortable—more comfortable, she had to confess, than the flat in which she expressed her own personality. If Venetia came to spend the night in London she was offered the choice of the sofa, or a nest made of outsize cushions, and the limited use of a bath which was covered during the day by equipment for developing photographs. Here at Senhouse Lindsay used a bathroom which the children did not often compete for; it was big enough to be a double bedroom, and carpeted; she would sit by the gas fire wrapped in a towel, reading. If she was hungry in the night she could help herself to biscuits from a Wedgwood barrel beside her bed, or make herself tea with the electric kettle; there was a chaise-longue to rest on, and a table provided with headed paper and ink for letter writing. It was a reminder to herself of her own personality, when Lindsay refrained from hanging up her jeans or putting away her underclothes, but left them where they fell. After the weeks she had spent at Senhouse, she feared the temptations of luxury.

Lindsay had arrived convalescent in November. She had been ill as a result of her own foolishness. She was a photographer, who worked on a permanent basis with her lover, Colin Trevor. Their way of life had been described in glowing terms in a recent colour supplement of a weekly newspaper. The feature had appeared months after the interviews were given and the information was out of date. At that time Lindsay and Colin lived in separate flats in a terraced house in Pimlico; he did investigative journalism and she illustrated it for papers which liked their features to be hard-hitting. The previous September Lindsay and Colin had gone to Africa intending to produce enough articles to pay for the trip, and a definitive book. In the autumn they had made what was intended to be a flying visit to London to do some selling and arrange some contracts. Lindsay had been told that she must take her anti-malaria pills for four weeks after her return; after three she was due her gap in taking the monthly dose of contraceptive pills, and, not needing the one, forgot the other. A week later, she was in the Hospital for Tropical Diseases with an acute form of one of the nastier varieties of malaria.

The flats were both let for a year, and even if Lindsay had been well enough to look after herself she had nowhere to go. Colin had gone back to Africa with many promises that she should follow with her camera later. But Lindsay knew that he had been speaking to one of her rivals, and knew too that this very rival was now away in some unspecified part of abroad. Colin kept writing to put off her return, urging her to prolong her convalescence.

Venetia claimed to be enchanted at the prospect of her sister's company for several months; Hugh, who had a strong sense of family obligation, seemed willing to welcome her too. Lindsay had arrived in time for Christmas.

At first the quiet and the comfort had been delicious. Lindsay relished lying neatly in a pink bed, and resting her eyes on the tranquil view. Venetia would bring her trays of food, set out in small tempting dishes; they would chat, or listen to music, and Venetia too appreciated the sickroom escape from the world's demands; she would sit on the window seat and get on with her tapestry, and

Lindsay would doze to the whisper of the wool against the canvas.

When had Lindsay started to feel that it was all too perfect? Gradually she would become irritated by the conformity of Venetia's life to the English dream. It was all too good to be true. Life was not really like this.

Lindsay was reminded of conversations in the sixth-form room at her school: all the girls whose minds should have been on Greek or physics devoted a good deal of their time to building castles in the air. It had depressed Lindsay, even then, that the others should have such conventional hopes. The common denominator of their aspirations was the rambling house in beautiful countryside, the neatly spaced, mixed-sex family, the dog, cat and motor car. At the time that she shared these discussions Lindsay had already seen such a life in action, for Venetia had been married for three years by then, and Lindsay used to stay with her and Hugh in the holidays. They had been in the lodge at the end of the drive then, where Hugh's mother now lived. The lodge matched the novelette's endings, and Lindsay had described their lives, only half-derisively, as Love's Young Dream. That had been all right, but she thought far from right the life that old Mr and Mrs Sennen lived at the big house, committed as it was to the keeping up of bountiful appearances on an income no longer large enough to support their obligations. When Mr Sennen died Lindsay had been in America, going through her fashion photography phase, and she came back to find Venetia installed, almost literally, in her mother-in-law's shoes, opening fêtes, sitting on public-spirited committees, chained, as it seemed to her sister, to the labour of an old-fashioned household. The years of baby-mess, which humanised even Hugh, had passed. Henry and Harriet were no longer of an age to provide excuses for leaving piles of laundry in the hall or stacks of unwashed plates on the draining-board. Venetia

71

and her twice-a-week charwoman were expected to reproduce the living once made gracious by three indoor and five outdoor staff. It infuriated Lindsay that her sister should be able to do so. She lay in her bed, now surrounded by her own personalised mess, and wondered how a sister of hers could be content to live as Venetia did, to pass her smug life collecting adipose tissue instead of ulcers, secure in virtue and affection.

Even old Mrs Sennen seemed to cast a slightly quizzical eye on her heirs. On her husband's death, she had moved out of the large house which had been her home for forty years, giving her children an almost indecently short time to pack up their belongings and transport them half a mile up the drive. Hugh had taken over the farm several years previously.

Now, when Lindsay visited her, as she did the next day with Venetia, she could never understand how a woman who had kept up a certain amount of state throughout her married life could so totally change her habits.

Venetia and Lindsay were asked to lunch, and they expected, rightly, that it would consist of a sliced loaf and some orange cheese, with margarine and instant coffee. It was Hugh's day for going to the market and he would eat in the pub.

Ann Sennen used one room of the three-roomed lodge, and slept and ate in it surrounded by assorted, dust-coated pictures and ornaments. Her divan bed was covered with a cheap Indian cloth, and her table by a tartan travelling rug. She cooked, rarely, on a bottled gas double burner. If the children brought her bunches of flowers she stuck them in a milk jug on the mantelpiece; Senhouse had been known for its spectacular flower arrangements in her day. She had kept her husband's spaniel till it died, but now she had only one cat. Her hair, once permed, she had cut by the village barber, in the same short style

72

as the older farm workmen, and she wore painters' smocks over trousers. In former centuries, she boasted, she would have been burnt as a witch. Hugh grumbled that his mother affected poverty to embarrass and annoy him, but Venetia said that she was just doing what she chose herself for the first time in a life dominated by first a bullying father, then a doting husband, whose feelings she could never bear to hurt.

The three women drank cider out of glasses given away at the garages where Mrs Sennen filled her pre-war open MG, having sold her estate car once she no longer needed to transport medical equipment for the Red Cross and other people's refuse for jumble sales. Venetia sat on a footstool and Lindsay and Mrs Sennen on the divan bed, and they had plates of food on their knees.

'Well, Venetia, how's the Red Cross, the parish council, the youth club and the friends of the Hale Hospital?' Ann Sennen said.

'Do you really want to know?' Venetia answered, smiling.

'No, darling, of course not, you know how I love not having to know. Don't tell me.'

'I always find it impossible to believe that Venetia really cares either,' Lindsay said, shifting the cat from the ticklish part of her thighs.

'It's part of the package,' Ann said. 'Isn't it, Venetia? Vegetable garden, deep freeze, and all that. The complete country life.'

'I couldn't bear it,' Lindsay exclaimed. 'Honestly, when I think that you were brought up in London, the same as I was. It gives me the creeps. When you were away with Hugh, two weekends ago, I thought I'd go stark staring mad. Of course they're not my children. But it wasn't them, they were quite good. But the feeling of that enormous pointless house—how many rooms do four people need to live in, for God's sake? And all that peace and quiet. Every time I opened the back door I thought there would be something like an army of rats waiting to attack me on the other side.'

'I thought you liked the country,' Ann Sennen said.

'Yes, so did I. And I don't mean to hurt your feelings, Venetia, it's lovely of you to have me here. But when it was the odd holiday with you, or weekends in Suffolk when Ma and Pa had that cottage, it all seemed quite different. I used to get off the train and take deep gulps of the air, and go into the house and sniff the wood fires and dogs and flowers, and feel quite overcome. I suppose it's because I've been here so long. I'm turning into the one who gets visited in the country instead of the one who does the visiting. Somehow I'd never realised that the life went on when it wasn't weekends and holidays.'

'Somebody has to provide the house and chop the wood and keep the dogs and grow the flowers. Not to mention buying the food and making the beds,' Venetia remarked mildly.

'Oh, I know, really I do. It's marvellous of you. All I mean is that it hadn't registered on me, not properly. Not till I really stuck it for these last months.'

'It sounds as though you're cured,' Ann Sennen said.

'Oh, I am, much better. And all thanks to Venetia doing all those things that I'm being so ungracious about. They're keeping me till midsummer, which is noble, and then I should be all right to go back to Africa.'

'Another three months.'

'We love having her,' Venetia said.

'Well, I hope you'll make use of me, go away for a holiday with Hugh or something.'

'That's sweet of you, but you know what Hugh is like about holidays.'

'I'm afraid he gets that from his father,' Ann Sennen remarked. 'Harry would never go away if he could help it. Staying with friends for shooting was about his limit. That's why I like travelling so much now, I've got a lot to catch up on.'

'I do envy you this trip,' Venetia sighed. 'The Mediterranean in the spring. The bliss of it.'

'Yes, I'm looking forward to it so much. Venetia, you will make sure that Harriet remembers about bringing food for the cat?'

'She won't forget. Anyway, Blackie's quite smart enough to walk up the drive for a second course. What clothes are you taking, Ann?'

'Nothing different. Smocks and trousers, and a caftan or two. I'm not the only eccentric on these cruises, darling, half the people there are as old and as dotty as I am.'

'I went on one once, to photograph Sir Dick Driver in action,' Lindsay said.

'Well then. You'll see too, Venetia, one day. When you're free.' Venetia stood up and started to collect the plates and mugs. She said,

'What an odd way of putting it.'

'Well, darling, if you follow in the footsteps of the earlier Sennens, you'll break out in old age. Did I ever tell you about my own mother-in-law, Lindsay? She took up ballooning when she was sixty-five. I rather regret that I shan't be there to see Venetia when she breaks out.'

'It's amazing how you've completely given up all the things you used to do,' Venetia said.

'You sound envious!' Lindsay said.

'Well, you see, I've retired. People don't seem to think that the sort of thing I spent my life doing was work that you could retire from. But for me it was a job, just as I think it is for you, Venetia, and very well you do it too, but it's as specific a commitment, really, as going out from nine to five. After all, someone has to do what we used to call public work, and all the more nowadays, when men

75

like Hugh can't spare the time. Henry was not so tied to to the farm, he could get away for committee meetings and the county council, it wasn't all so one sided, but Venetia has to do it for the two of them even without the staff we used to have.'

'Venetia doesn't have to do it,' Lindsay argued. 'She must like it.'

'Yes, well, I liked it too. As far as I know you like your work, don't you, Lindsay? But it's none the less work for all that.'

'But you make it sound so archaic, feudal almost. As though the people who live round here couldn't manage if Mrs Sennen from Senhouse wasn't there running things. It's as bad as handing round port wine and broth. It's a different world, don't you see?' Lindsay said, thinking how Colin Trevor would retch at Mrs Sennen's attitude.

'Of course they'd manage. Anyway most of what Venetia does isn't so localised. You don't have one charitable lady per parish backed up by the vicar's daughters these days. But I can tell you, Lindsay, if you had no husband and no money you'd be very glad of the gift of a cot for the baby or the loan of a pram. Or when you were in hospital, didn't you welcome the library trolley? Who do you think was pushing it along? Girls like Venetia. Or if you were the wife of a prisoner, wouldn't you be glad of a crèche to leave the baby in while you visited your man behind bars?'

'Well, but in a welfare state—'

'Yes, but the state doesn't provide. Maybe it should, but till it does Venetia and other people like her who take on these boring chores, unpaid, are worth their weight. Just because I've retired from it, don't imagine that I deny the value of the work I spent my life doing.'

'If the state takes over it'll be me out of a job, that's for sure,' Venetia said. 'Who'd employ me, for God's sake?'

'There's teaching,' Lindsay said weakly, and Venetia did

not answer. She had left school with moderate exam results, and after a year of enjoying herself at her father's expense, had got a job teaching in a very expensive pre-preparatory school in London, where the classes were so small and the children so well brought up that her pragmatic methods and nervous discipline seemed adequate. In fact the children loved her. But the affection of her former pupils was no reference in the stony eyes of a county education committee, and she and Lindsay both knew perfectly well that she had no hope of getting a teaching job within reach of Senhouse.

Ann Sennen started pruning the plants in a bottle garden, with delicate snips of her long-bladed tools. A scent suddenly reminiscent of tropical heat and vegetation floated across the room, and Lindsay breathed it in, thinking sharply about Colin Trevor.

'I had a letter from Dorothy Westbourne, Venetia,' Ann Sennen said. 'She wants to come over and have lunch.'

'Which one is she, Ann?'

'You know, Gilbert's second wife. The one who is such a keen collector. I had to promise her she could see the cases at Senhouse again. But she isn't coming till a fortnight after I get back, so you needn't bother to do any dusting, I'll see to it.'

'Does anyone ever look at your showcases?' Lindsay asked.

'No, never. They can't have been dusted for two years, I'd say.'

'Why do you keep the stuff? It must be quite valuable.'

'I did suggest that Hugh should sell some of the things, after Henry died. But you know Hugh! I suppose they make a good nest egg, at least. Venetia darling, you look exhausted. Was your day in London too much for you?'

When it was school holidays Venetia was usually unable to attend the magistrates' court, but this year Lindsay was at Senhouse to cope with Henry and Harriet, who actually spent most of the day 'helping' on the farm. Venetia left her car for Lindsay to use, and in the afternoon Lindsay told Hugh with the firmness of one who was not his wife that he was to take charge of the children, and she drove into Halemouth to pick up her sister. The court was still in session. Lindsay slipped into the back of the room. She was interested in a side of Venetia's life that was new to her, and marvelled again at the difference that there could be between two sisters. The only place in the court in which she could ever imagine herself was the dock.

Venetia sat on the right of the chairman of the bench. Lindsay stiffened at the sight of him. Hypocrite, she thought, damned hypocrite. The week before she had noticed on the local television news that he had sent a man to prison for interfering with a fifteen-year-old girl. He ought to be stopped, everyone must know about him.

When Lindsay was fourteen Colonel Wilton had put his tweedy arm around her waist, pressed his gin-soaked lips against her cheek, mumbled endearments which she had found more unexpected than disgusting at the time. When she was eighteen, on another visit to Senhouse, she'd heard, without much interest, Ann Sennen's sorrowful, but taking-for-granted references to his unfortunate liking for little girls. He was one of her oldest friends, a retired officer almost too much like his archetype to be credible; he lived near Halemouth and was chairman of the Conservatives, a county councillor, a district councillor, a deputy lord-lieutenant, the whole package. It would never have done for him to be revealed as a pathetic, dirty old man. And as Ann Sennen remarked, nobody could have guessed that the Andrews girl was only thirteen.

When Lindsay was twenty she noticed a report of one of his speeches about the lax morals of the young and the permissive generation, and read it aloud at dinner. Venetia laughed. Why was Lindsay so worked up about it, she asked. He never really did any harm. Lindsay protested; hypocrisy, cant, humbug, she brought out all her own generation's favourite perjoratives.

'So long as he isn't found out,' Venetia had said, amused. 'That's the eighth deadly sin, didn't you know?'

'I've got a lot of time for the old man,' Hugh had remarked. 'He's good on the bench, just what's needed.' Venetia had not yet become a magistrate at that time. 'After all, someone's got to send the young layabouts to jug and ban the blue films. It's an administrative necessity. You could have a computer dishing out the law just as well. I can't see that it matters if he isn't holier than thou. You aren't a saint, dear sister-in-law.'

'No, and I don't tell other people to be either,' Lindsay exclaimed. She'd left Senhouse still fuming, and spoken a lot to her friends in London about the sanctimonious bourgeoisie.

Lindsay now felt like leaping to her feet and denouncing the man. She wondered whether the other magistrate, a tired, thin man with a row of pens in his breast pocket, knew about him.

There was a vase of tulips on the magistrates' table. Venetia was wearing a purple tweed suit, and a soup plate hat. She looked attentive and serious. Lindsay thought in sudden terror, That's a middle-aged woman. Would eight years transform her too? She glanced down at her own clothes and reminded herself that she need not give way to the years. No, Venetia had dressed to fit her part. She was not really the person that she looked from the back of the court.

But what could the accused woman think of her judge? She was a collapsingly fat woman who must be the same age as Venetia, but whose life had been harder. She had obviously dressed up, and was wearing a scarlet skirt in a shiny fabric, which came well above her knees. She probably regarded Venetia as a symbol of the society which oppressed her. The solicitor had mentioned that she earned a bit by going out cleaning. The women who employed her and the enemy set up to judge her, all secure in their certainty of the next meal for themselves and their children, all free to squander the sums of money which were meaningless to them and an hour's back-break to her—how she must hate them. Lindsay would never employ domestic help. Even when Venetia's twice-a-week lady came, driving her car and with her hair freshly set, Lindsay was burdened by the resentment which she would have felt herself at having to clean another woman's bath. Even if the woman did not hate her, Lindsay felt, she should.

There was no argument about the facts of the case. Mrs Mahon had been caught with a bag full of goods she had not paid for. She'd had some money in her purse, but her solicitor said it was earmarked for the rent. There were silences and mumbles and whispered discussions. Throughout it all Mrs Mahon looked as though it had nothing to do with her. Lindsay thought how she must feel, that 'they' had taken over. She would be told what to do, when to move or sit down or make her ritual expressions of regret. Apparently it was by no means the first time that she had appeared before this bench. But what was she to do? It was implied, well known by everyone in the room, that she had no choice. The family could be clothed from stalls at jumble sales and fed on scrag end; but if Shelagh needed the right dress for the school play, or Brian would miss the form outing by charabanc if he could not contribute his fare, Mrs Mahon had to find the money somehow. Anyway, the supermarket could spare the sum, pathetically small as it was, better than the Mahon family.

How could Venetia bring herself to sit there, her crocodile bag bulging on the table in front of her, and not pull out some notes to pay for Mrs Mahon's stolen goods? Is she thinking, Lindsay wondered, there but for the luck of the draw I'd be?

She asked Venetia on the way home. 'I don't see how she can possibly not do it again, she'll have to.'

'I expect you're right.' Venetia had thrown her hat in the back of the car, an instantly rejuvenating gesture, and concentrated on the driving mirror; for a magistrate, she had told Lindsay before, it was almost worse to be copped for speeding than for scooping a lamp post.

'You must feel such a hypocrite, putting her on probation, passing judgment on people like that wretched woman. I mean, how can you?'

'Someone's got to do it, I suppose.'

'Yes, but not us. Well damn it, I'd steal if my kids were hungry, wouldn't you? Who are we to—? Anyway, the shops shouldn't make it so easy. It serves them right, they ask for it. I've even done it by mistake myself—you know, put something in my bag. Luckily I've always noticed it in time and paid, but I can see how these harassed middle-aged housewives get it wrong.'

'Only by mistake?' Venetia said.

'What do you mean—? Oh I see. Yes, dear sister, only by mistake. I'm not reduced to the breadline yet. But I can see how I might do it on purpose, and I suppose that's something you'll never understand, not living the kind of life you do. You're too rich.'

'Well, darling, you're not exactly poor.'

'No,' Lindsay said defensively. 'But I know what it's like to be poor. After all, my friends are like Colin, working class.'

Lindsay and Venetia had been brought up in the security of a professional home with a moneyed background. By the time Lindsay was in her teens, Venetia and their brother Simon had left home, and lavished on Lindsay were the comforts accorded to a girl who was in the position of the only child of elderly parents. She felt enclosed and oppressed by their attention, and bored by her freedom to share their occupations. She would have preferred to be in the schoolroom with another child, rather than be invited to their dinner parties and taken with them to theatres and galleries. Weekends in their cottage, unless she had a friend of her own age to stay, had been, she used to say, purgatory.

Doctor Fell dropped dead on his rounds one day when Lindsay was twenty, not yet of an age to see her parents as individuals, or to sympathise with their problems. Venetia had tried to make her kinder to Mrs Fell, but Lindsay could or would not understand that people of her parents' age could regret the gulf between their youthful aspiration and elderly reality. Lindsay could still say, 'I won't be like that when I'm old', and not suppose for a moment that her life would fail to turn out as planned. When Venetia reminded her that Mrs Fell would have preferred a different environment to that of the wife of a doctor with a London practice, Lindsay felt more impatient than sympathetic, and determined all the more strongly that her own life would be what she made it.

Ralph Fell had been a general practitioner who lived and worked in Kensington, between the slums to the north and the south. He did one day a week at the local hospital where his poorer patients went; the others usually arranged to be treated in one of the teaching hospitals. He was the son of a long line of doctors in the district of Norfolk where his wife's family had been squires. Iris Fell's ancestors had been at Blenheim, Waterloo and Sevastopol, her father at Mafeking, her brother at the Somme. Her relatives included Members of Parliament and uncontroversial bishops, the heirs of generations of farming squires and hunting parsons; a several times great-grandfather had complained at the reforms of agriculture suggested by Coke of Norfolk, and his son had copied them. Iris had married for love and accepted the urban life her husband's career enforced with traditional stoicism. Yet there was unspoken in the children's upbringing the implication that this was all a substitute for the ideal existence, in which, though she did not, Iris Fell's relations would live in a place she would teach Simon, Venetia and Lindsay to regard as home. The house became a convalescents' hostel after the Second World War. But in a better world, the Fells would have lived lavishly under wide eastern skies, surrounded by fertile arable acres; their natural state should be to run wild as children and to rule a rural community as adults.

Lindsay went to the same London day school that Venetia had attended, but the power of conventional upbringing was weaker by then, or perhaps the Fells' authority diminished with age. Venetia had been to a garden party at Buckingham Palace and to a couple of coming-out dances given for the daughters of her mother's friends. Lindsay giggled at the idea of doing anything of the kind, and found her entertainment in dark cellars with people who did not enquire which schools new acquaintances had been to.

Venetia remembered, even if she did not obey, the rules

that clothes could be cheap but shoes and gloves must be good; that no lady painted her nails or dyed her hair or went on a bus without paying the fare. Lindsay had never learnt them. She told Venetia once that one of her boy friends had said that Venetia was the embryo of the women he saw on the other side of the counter at Harrods' Christmas shopping rush. One day he said, Venetia would have blue hair and a poodle and her elegant thin legs would be shod in regularly polished leather; she would wear hats and play bridge and the only printed information her eyes would rest on would be the pages of the *Daily Telegraph*. Venetia had been mortified, especially because the youth had described, without knowing her, Mrs Fell. Yet her elder daughter at least understood that it was not how Iris Fell would have liked to be. She lived an expedient life; but her spiritual home was a country garden where she dead-headed the roses wearing a floppy hat, and dealt generously and tactfully with the problems of a small village.

'You have the sort of life Ma would have liked to lead,' Lindsay said.

Venetia negotiated a roundabout with verve. 'Had you never noticed?'

'No, I think it used to seem much more the rural idyll, when I came for the odd day. It's only being here for so long that brings it home to me what it's like. It seems rather sad.'

'Thanks very much.'

'When I was a kid, it always seemed so perfect and romantic, the way you and Hugh got married and lived in your little grey home in the west with roses round the door.'

'What's changed then?'

'I suppose it's the house, really. It's so depressingly permanent. I'd go mad if I thought I'd live in the same

84

place for keeps. And you lead such a grown-up life. Like people's mothers. You used to be much more—well, gay and adventurous.'

They were driving along the stretch of road which went through Halegate Forest; the homegoing traffic had thinned out, and it was too early in the year for many caravans. The road ahead was striped in the evening sun with the shadow of the oak trees, and the fresh leaves were almost transparent green. Venetia pulled the car into an area of flattened earth, littered with the debris of many picnics. She got out and walked a little way down a grassy ride between the trees and Lindsay followed her. They sat side by side on a mossy fallen trunk. Venetia scratched the tip of her sensible brown shoe against her other ankle. She said, 'What do you think happens to gaiety and adventure when there are children around?'

'I don't see what that's got to do with it,' Lindsay said.

'It has, though. After all, tell me a thriller where an active heroine has children—dependent ones, anyway. The two are incompatible. You get earthbound.'

'Oh Venetia, that's an excuse. Why, wherever I've been in the world there have been people travelling with their babies, in carry-cots or slings—anything really. It's only a question of wanting to.'

'Yes, well, you can't do that if your husband has to make sure there's someone there to milk the cows every morning at six o'clock. No, I'm afraid that the tradition of the story ending at the altar had more sense to it than I ever thought. It's all right at first, having the wedding-ring just makes life seem more adventurous, even one little baby you can tote around with you quite easily, skiing holidays, going out in the boat. We used to despise people who made their children the excuse for not doing things, Henry came along with us, I fed him myself, no mess or fuss, it all seemed so easy. It was Harriet that hit me. Two of them just are

85

not as portable as one. And Henry was mobile by then, and talking and being a bother, and Harriet was a frightful baby, she seemed to cry all the time. And Hugh got so solemn. Lots of my friends have said the same, actually, it seems to overcome fathers when the second one is born, there's a real commitment to responsibility, years of having to provide the food and clothes and heat and toys and everything else.'

'But you don't have to become quite such a stick in the mud.'

'Tell me the alternative. I'd like to know what you'd do with two small kids in tow. And I don't mean the hippy trail to Afghanistan or Nepal, either.'

'I think you're just making the children your excuse for your attitude of mind.'

'I'll be interested to see if you say the same when you're in that position, that's all,' Venetia said crossly. They sat in silence for a few minutes. Lindsay explored the tactile refinements of the twigs, dust, acorns and leaves under her feet. She picked up an empty cigarette packet in her toes and dropped it into a wire litter-bin. 'I suppose,' Venetia said thoughtfully, 'it's really because one's so afraid.'

'What do you mean?'

'Once you have children you get terrified of everything. I don't mean just losing your nerve for driving fast or mountain climbing, but getting overcome by terror of things that happen to other people. I don't hear the news of a single crash, explosion or epidemic without trembling because I visualise the children in them. Sometimes I stay awake at night rigid with fear because of the dangers they'll have to face when they leave home. Hugh thinks I'm demented, I daren't tell him anymore when I get like that. But I think all my friends with kids are the same. And that's what dishes a woman's spirit of adventure. And you think I'm staid and dull—but just wait till you have two or three children and see if you feel like the daredevil of the lower fourth then.'

'Actually I have thought that you are a bit over-protective of Henry and Harriet.'

'Oh for God's sake.' Venetia stood up and walked briskly towards the car. 'I've often thought I'd have liked your sort of life. But given what I'm landed with, surely I do something right? I'm not that bad.'

'If I can't tell you where you're wrong, who can?'

'Criticism should be constructive. You are just carping.'

'Well, I'm sorry,' Lindsay said, a little huffily. She and her group had always prided themselves on accepting an outsider's view of their behaviour. They knew themselves to be armoured by instinct, they applied their brains to their work—and Lindsay's friends were successful career girls—and they gave emotion full swing in their love lives. Having eliminated considerations of property and of propriety from their unions, stable, in the lawyer's phrase, or otherwise, they were free to concentrate on their hearts. Common sense, they expected, would govern eventual marriage. But that would be much later.

In the past Lindsay had not criticised her sister's way of life. This was partly because for many years Venetia had seemed too much her elder sister, completely of another generation, and partly because of Venetia's envious joking about Lindsay's life. And in more recent years, Lindsay's visits to Senhouse had been so brief that she had not taken in the details of life there, and had in any case been treated as a visitor. Now that she understood the pattern, had seen the Sennen family's life from the inside, she felt impatient and depressed at what she saw. Surely, she thought, it need not be inevitable for the spirited, dashing girl she remembered Venetia to have been to succumb. She gave the impression of being in fetters of duty and convention and expedience, and could, with a little encouragement, break out. It was impossible for Lindsay's sister to believe in the life she led. She wore perfect camouflage, merged into the background of the country lady who performed what was expected of her at home and in public, and even—for the Sennens preserved most family traditions—in church, but Lindsay was convinced that she was acting a part which had become literally her second nature.

'Anyway,' Venetia said as she turned the car into the drive past Ann Sennen's cottage, 'what could I do? In practical terms?'

'Well, you're free and over twenty-one. You could go away.'

'Apart from that.'

'Yes, I suppose adventure is a bit unlikely in the circumstances. Well, have a boy friend, for a start.'

'I,' Venetia said, 'am happily married.'

She got out of the car and went round to the back for her parcels. 'Stop it, Lindsay, you're not to carry things. No, I mean it. You're not supposed to, not while you are still convalescent. Here, take my handbag.' Venetia heaved a cardboard box full of groceries up, and Lindsay went to open the back door for her. The dog came out, barking and wagging his tail, and the children shouted from the sitting-room where they were watching television.

'Return of the châtelaine,' Lindsay muttered. The children's dirty plates from tea were still on the table, and Venetia pushed them to one side with the bottom of the box to clear a space to put it down. The door of the refrigerator was hanging open, and the heavy cover over one of the Aga's hotplates was raised. Venetia started to clear up without comment.

Lindsay went straight to her bedroom. She flung herself on the bed, and pushed her wooden sandals off with the footboard so that they thumped on to the floor. A purple

88

and blue picture of a woman and a child had been propped on her bedside table, and she reached out for the naïve drawing. On the back Harriet had written 'I wish you would stay with us for ever and ever'. Lindsay rolled over on her stomach and fumbled in the back of the drawer of the small mahogany table. She had to get up to find some matches, but they were where efficient Venetia had left them, beside the china candlestick on the mantelpiece, provided in case of power cuts. She wondered why they didn't lay on life-jackets and shrouds while they were about it. She edged the dried leaf into the paper with skilful movements of her long, dirty fingers and lit the cigarette with a deep sigh, the sweet, heavy smell filled the room.

By the time that Venetia had cleared the children's tea, made and cleared their supper, cooked dinner for the grown-ups, set out platefuls for the dog and the cats, chivvied Harriet to take the outside leaves of the cabbage to her guinea pigs and Henry to clean his shoes for the next day, put out of reach the electric toaster which caused the mains electric switch to trip when it was used, relaid the drawing-room fire which there had not been time to do in the morning, decanted a new bottle of sherry and rung back three people who had left telephone messages for her, Lindsay had smoked and relaxed and, as she called it, unknotted herself. When Venetia knocked at her door she was still on the bed, but poised to rise and change into a garment which Hugh would dislike at least marginally less at his dinner table than denim jeans.

Venetia put her head round the door. 'Dinner in quarter of an hour,' she said. She came in, her nostrils a little dilated. 'I say, what a funny—oh, Lindsay, you haven't—' she turned quickly and shut the door behind her. Then she went to the window and opened it as widely as she could. Lindsay took off her shirt and her trousers, and stood with her back to the room, choosing a dress. The mirror on the inside of the wardrobe door showed her sallow body. She wore only a brief pair of pants, and she could see the reflection of Venetia glancing away. She reached for a long cheese-cloth smock and pulled it over her head.

'I'm decent now,' she said. Venetia picked up the sandals and put them together under a chair; she started to fold the towel which had been crumpled in a heap on the floor.

'That's the first time you've done that,' she said.

'I guess I can do with it.'

'Ought you to? Your health, I mean?'

'They only said not to drink.'

'It wouldn't have occurred to them to tell you about the other thing, you must know that. I mean, after all, whatever you do with your own friends, even if you do take it for granted, it's still illegal. Hugh could go to prison for letting you smoke in our house.'

'He won't know, will he?'

'Well, I could. Go to prison, that is. I won't tell him.'

'I should think he'd be quite glad of an excuse to turn me out of the house.'

'Oh, you know he isn't like that. Though I don't know what he'd say if he knew— Darling, must you, really? Is it necessary?'

'As necessary as that large sherry you're about to go and pour out for yourself, and does less harm to my liver. You should try it.' Venetia sat down beside her sister on the bed, their reflections in the mirror they faced misleadingly alike, and reached out for the old tobacco tin. Gingerly she prised the lid up and smelled the pungent contents.

'I must say, I have sometimes wondered—' she said slowly. Then she snapped the box shut and thrust it at Lindsay. 'Hide the damned thing, for God's sake. I've got

90

enough to cope with without being copped for that. And don't let the children see it.'

Lindsay went to wash. She found Harriet in the bath, and Henry modestly clad in pyjama trousers foaming at the mouth at the basin.

'He used half the tube,' Harriet said.

'So did I when I was his age,' Lindsay replied. She could remember doing that kind of thing so clearly that she had often wondered how Venetia could forget, as her prohibitions and scoldings showed that she had. She sat on the stool beside the bath and watched Harriet making patterns on the wall with the bath bubbles. The child's pigtails stuck out at right angles to her bright cheeks. The skin on her body was downy and tender and, though she was thin, looked bonelessly soft. I wouldn't like Colin to see her like this, Lindsay thought. Even I can hardly keep my hands from fondling her. She tried to remember her own body changing from its sexless immaturity to the experienced instrument it had become; had its skin really grown thinner and its bones harder? She felt her first terror of increasing age.

My lifestyle has made me think myself young, she thought, staring at her face in the glass and seeing flaws she had never noticed. When Venetia was as old as I am she had two children and all this. I'm twenty-six and I count as a girl, but soon it will show that I'm not. I've behaved as though the world passes on and I don't change. Yet there are my friends to prove that my youth isn't eternal, of my boy friends two are married with families and one is dead. I shall turn into a middle-aged woman and desperate eyes will peer from beneath this hair, a wrinkled smile will deny the years.

She thought of the women she had admired who seemed indifferent to the fact that their faces framed by the latest clothes showed that they did not belong to the generation which had invented them, like the deputy editor of the first newspaper which had employed her. Perhaps they had believed in the image they chose to present, perhaps they had not minded because they had not believed in their age, but had felt themselves to be as old as their lifestyles.

I don't want to be like that, she thought; but I may be a little like that already. It was nothing to do with marriage and children, the editor had three of each, and the photographer was married too. It was something to do with the picture one carried of oneself in one's mind and matched against reflections in a mirror or in people's eyes, something to do with being accepted at one's own estimation. If the clothes were those of a rebel from middle-age convention and the attitudes those of a generation which was beginning, perhaps, to drop a little way into society again, then it was a girl wearing them, not a woman. And so long as no comparison was made with someone whom the calendar showed to be a girl the approximation would go on being convincing.

Lindsay watched Venetia over the candlelit dinner table. There was soup, grilled fish which Venetia had bought in Halemouth in the lunchtime recess, and runner beans from the last summer's deep-frozen crop. The Cheddar and Stilton cheeses had been sent from farms near their native villages. Venetia wore a grey jersey with a floor-length tweed skirt, and listened politely as Hugh told her about the day's work on the farm; a dog had been worrying sheep, the tractor driver had spent all day stripping down an engine which Hugh was sure had been in perfect order, the cowman's wife said he had flu. Venetia meticulously peeled an apple, dropping transparent slivers of skin on her plate. Was hers the invariable fate, Lindsay asked herself, of married women? Surely she was not obliged to marry a way of life with her husband? Perhaps, Lindsay thought, he makes up for it in bed.

92

That was the sort of topic which Lindsay did not hesitate to discuss with her own friends. They had grown up when the freedoms of the nineteen sixties were being revealed in girls' schools, and supposed that they were the first generation to be able to admit even the fact that women menstruated, let alone that unmarried girls made love to their boyfriends. Venetia, years ago, had told her teenage sister that probably three-quarters of her own contemporaries did so, but all of them would make every effort to conceal it from their most intimate friends. They made a parade of chastity, and had hypocritical conversations discussing what 'it' must be like. Not, Venetia had sadly said, that 'it' had probably been up to much for her friends, with at least half their attention concentrated on the danger of discovery. It must have been almost worse to be expected to enjoy it in those circumstances than to be doing one's bit by lying back and thinking of England. And to fear once a month that fate was poised to punish you—thank goodness for the Pill, and for its fail-safe; Lindsay had been through one abortion herself.

'I think my suggestion of finding a boy friend is what you should do,' she said, when Hugh had gone to watch a Western and the two women were sitting with coffee in the drawing-room. Hugh had lit the fire with his single match, and Venetia tossed some pine cones from a copper bucket into its red centre.

'Why are you so determined to change my life? I can't see what you think is wrong with it,' Venetia said defensively.

'Oh darling, so staid, so dull. You're middle-aged, and you needn't be. The house, the village, the magistrates' court—'

'You're only seeing the externals. Hugh, Henry and Harriet is what you should say.'

'But aren't you bored? Don't you long to break out?'

93

'I think what you mean is that you're getting bored, now you are not ill anymore. You never did like the country much.'

'But Venetia—well, like those old jokes used to say—when did the romance go out of your marriage? I mean, Hugh doesn't exactly behave like a ball of fire any more.'

'Well, what is a ball of fire? Someone who is good in bed and a dead loss out of it.'

'At least you get a thrill where you need it.'

'It's not worth it. Five minutes' pleasure and a hell of a life—no thanks.' Venetia spoke with sudden vigour. 'There aren't any knights on galloping chargers, if they stick around they turn into men with a bilious attack who want to be waited on. Or they talk about love in a cottage and don't ask who is going to get the cesspit emptied. All for the sake of some fun in bed. No, the trouble with people like you is that you believe the two things necessarily go together—you're the romantic. I never was.'

'Darling, are you talking from experience?'

'I know what I'm talking about. You're muddling up love and liking and sexual compatibility. No wonder your own life gets into such a mess. After all,' Venetia went on, a worm turning, 'there's Colin out in Africa with what's her name and you're so twitched about what they are doing together you can hardly hide it. What sort of relationship is that for you and him to have? And what about all the last few—Christopher, and Grenville, and—what was he called—Ferdinand? Was that true love every time? You always thought it was more than just fun in bed.'

Lindsay said stung, 'You'd realise what it meant if you had.'

'Damn you, Lindsay, it's just because I have that I do know how little it means compared with what Hugh—' Venetia stopped speaking abruptly, and turned away to poke the fire. She pushed a smouldering log on to the flames, and shook her stinging fingers sharply in the air. 'I've burnt myself.'

Lindsay felt the triumph she remembered from her childhood when her schoolgirl needling had at last provoked Venetia into admitting what she had refused to discuss with a kid sister.

'So there has been someone else,' she exclaimed. 'But you always told me that Hugh was the one and only—do you mean that you've recently—?'

'I don't mean anything at all and it's nothing to do with you.'

'Does Hugh know? Was it someone who lives round here?'

'For God's sake shut up.' Venetia turned on her sister, her face flushed and her eyes sparkling. Her hair was tousled and with the mask of sensible calm slipped she looked quite different from the woman who coped with the minutiae of gracious living.

'I'm so glad.' Lindsay slipped her arm round Venetia's shoulder, though it was unusual for them to touch one another. 'I won't go on about it. But it worried me to think of you wasting your life. I'm going to bed.'

'I'm not wasting my life, and it's not as dull as you seem determined to think.'

Lindsay shook out the cushions and placed them at the proper angle on the sofa. It was the first time she had done anything at Senhouse on the list of what she thought of as unnecessary frills. Venetia lit a cigarette, and poured herself some cognac. 'There,' Lindsay said, 'think of your liver and your lungs. Much better to break the law like me.' She went upstairs, and ran herself a bath. Colin would think she was scraggy now; her ribs showed, but her body, though thin, was wide. Even her breasts had shrunk, she had lost so much weight. Colin and that girl, together

95

in Africa ... if only he didn't know that she was virtually in a nunnery. She wished she could make him as jealous as she was.

Lindsay got off the bus in Halemouth and looked de-
jectedly around. There had been a letter from her mother
this morning, happy to think of her daughters together,
ecstatic about the luxury and warmth of Cape Town.
Lindsay decided for at least the twentieth time that she
would not go out there, and, her mind following well-
worn tracks, that she could not get her tenants out of the
London flat, and that staying with other friends would be
no better than being with Venetia, and much less comfortable. There had been another delaying note from Colin
that morning.

'What is there to do in the country?' she had said in
despair at breakfast. Venetia was making lists of telephone
calls, shopping and errands. Hugh had come in for what
was his mid-morning coffee, and refrained from comment,
though the glance he gave her before raising *The Times*
in front of his face again was expressive.

'The doctors did tell you to go for walks,' Venetia
suggested.

'I've been for walks,' Lindsay said. She had trudged,
marched or trailed round the gardens, up the drive, along
the public footpaths; through muddy fields, under dripping
trees, over slimy stiles, inflexibly unattracted by the
solaces of nature. It was not that she could not see the
flowers, birds and vistas; her eyesight was excellent, and
her photographer's sense of mass and form, of grouping
and detail, had always been praised. But there were people

97

to whom a conservationist's dream landscape, unpeopled and untouched by man, represented a kind of hell. Lindsay had performed commissions in open country, and a series she did once of stone and brick walls, showing the different textures and techniques of construction, had even won a prize. But she only felt at home in a landscape of streets and buildings. She required the sight of strange faces, and admired Hogarth more than Constable. In fact, one of her cherished projects was to do a portfolio of twentieth-century London faces, crowded together at greyhound races or on underground platforms. 'I like people,' she said crossly. 'Human relationships—they are what matter to me. That's why I prefer towns.'

'Mm.' Venetia returned to her mail, which seemed to consist of brown envelopes containing duplicated sheets of the minutes of meetings or requests for subscriptions. Then she glanced up. 'You know if you have a wound and the place starts itching when it's nearly better? That's what's wrong with you. You feel restless, you are itching mentally.'

'I'd willingly scratch her,' Hugh muttered.

'I suppose you are right,' Lindsay said. 'I am being a bore and you are kind to put up with me.' She thought, as several times before, how much she would like to be able to relieve the Sennens of the burden of putting up with her.

'I'm sorry I can't keep you company on your walk,' Venetia said. 'I must do my round for the Alexandra Rose Day. Unless you'd like to come too.'

'I can see it,' Lindsay said; Venetia in her matching skirt and jersey, her patterned silk headscarf, her unflagging, brogue-shod feet, and Lindsay in her pre-Raphaelite dress of faded velvet, her hair trailing, her fur coat mangy with its bare patches. 'I don't think they'd donate to me.'

Venetia said, 'I could drive you somewhere.'

98

'No, I'll catch the bus. Drop me at the end of the drive.'

'Oh good, if you're going to Halemouth you might pick up some worm pills at the vet!' The idea of worm pills amused Lindsay, and she caught the bus cheerfully. Worm pills! They epitomised, somehow, her picture of Venetia's life. Marriage, she thought, would not reduce her to having to turn her mind to worm pills.

Halemouth, though it was the county town, was not sufficiently urban to make up to Lindsay for the tedium of the country around it. The bus terminus was beside the central car park, an acre of concrete where there had once been a garden, surrounded by the usual shops which prove to a visitor that he has reached the town centre. Lindsay strolled into Woolworth and Marks & Spencer, consoled by their familiar atmosphere of bright, cheap, clean uniformity. She bought a shopping basket and a bag of apples. The shops and the streets were not full; after the Easter holidays, before the season for day-trippers, Halemouth in light May sunshine ought to be delightful for the discerning traveller. But I'm vulgar, Lindsay thought, literally; I like places crowded. There were some expensive cars going slowly along the street, clean and bearing the badges of motoring organisations; most contained one middle-aged couple; and the woman passenger had guide books open on her lap. Lindsay could remember going on outings like that with her parents, sulking behind them as they brightly commended ancient monuments to her notice, refusing the wholesome food they offered her in White Harts, Red Lions, Blue Boars or Green Men.

I've always been the difficult youngest child, she thought, always trailing in achievement and estimation behind Simon, the satisfactory son, who had passed examinations when he should and got into father's own medical school, chosen a speciality both respectable and lucrative, and settled with his American wife in Glasgow; behind

99

Venetia, pretty and co-operative, who made so ideal, so dream-fulfilling a marriage. No wonder that Ralph and Iris Fell had failed to conceal a worried disappointment in their youngest daughter, who seemed an everlasting ugly duckling, who only got two O Levels and refused to take a secretarial course, whose private life, although they tried their utmost not to know its details, was blatantly embarrassing. But I'm the one who lives in the present, Lindsay defiantly reminded herself; I don't try to preserve a dead way of life. Venetia's the dodo, not me.

It was difficult to live in a world which neither shared nor recognised her values, but in which she was an outsider whose eccentricities were deprecated, whose achievements were meaningless. The society was hypocritical and dying, of that she was convinced, but when she had seen no other for so long it became difficult to reject its values. Her teenage rebellions had always been bolstered by friendly accomplices.

Take, for instance, Venetia's behaviour about the smoking. Her resignation, her apparent acceptance that Lindsay dared where she did not, but her obvious preference not to know, all this had made Lindsay uneasy, and spoiled her pleasure since that episode three weeks before. If only she had been angry Lindsay would have gladly defied her. After all, in Lindsay's circle, smoking tobacco was seen as a surrender to money values. Any lift was marred by knowing how it contributed to the revenues of government and big business. Lindsay's friends had accepted intellectually the releases in all the reports since Baroness Wootton's, and felt justified in what they had almost forgotten was breaking the law. But these arguments were unnecessary with Venetia and impossible with Hugh, who would not listen, or if he had to hear, would laugh. His attitude, Lindsay always felt, was very much like his grandfather's must have been, that women should be left to get on with things in their own sphere. He rarely, as far as she could see, intruded, or even allowed himself to be welcomed into it. And that was another thing that was wrong with life at Senhouse. Lindsay missed the company of men.

She stood on the pavement and looked glumly around. Of all the unenticing townscapes she had ever seen, this one took the cake, with its unremarkable shops and houses, indistinguishable from any other English town just within commuter reach of London. It had once been a port, when the river was navigable. It was now too silted up to be used for any boat with more draught than a rowing skiff, and the quays and wharves which might have retained a certain melancholy grandeur had been turned into car parks. The town centre, such as it was, consisted of a war memorial. Tattered remains of the poppy wreaths which had been laid there six months before still fluttered on its granite steps. The statue was a sentimental portrayal of a young soldier, his arms at an angle which could never have supported the weight of his rifle, his lips drawn back in a grin, which could not, presumably, have been intended to look murderous.

Attached to the stone were some fine examples of modern street furniture; a warning of a roundabout ahead, a sign setting out the hours when street parking was permitted, and a direction arrow to the town's information bureau.

Lindsay followed along the road and found that the information bureau was a glass-walled booth in the entrance of the town hall, in which a woman sat surrounded by pamphlets, leaflets, printed cards and volumes of timetables. On a notice board outside it were advertised entertainments like the Halemouth Amateur Dance Band's Gala Night, and the Cine Club's Festival of Holiday Films made by its members. Lindsay read that she could attend classes to learn how to bind books, keep fit or do folk weaving, or that she might join the Chapel Women's Bright Hour, or unstructured meditation in the Women's Institute Hall once a fortnight. Householders who had not paid their rates would be summoned, and there was to be an open meeting of the ratepayers' protest group in the town hall that evening.

Lindsay bought a guide book and map from the woman, and glanced through it, untempted by the attractions it described, from bowling greens to flower clocks.

She moved to one side as a man came up the steps and tapped on the window of the information bureau.

'Can I help you?' the woman asked.

'I'm not sure. It's difficult, sounds a bit silly really.' He opened his briefcase and fumbled in it. As he bent over, his sagging stomach was dented by the rigid leather of his belt, and the buttons of his shirt gaped to show the swelling skin. He produced a book and handed it to the woman behind the window, and said, 'I don't suppose you —well, you'll probably think I'm mad. But can you tell me—is there anywhere round here with a monument like the one in the cover picture?' Through the glass Lindsay saw a gaudy book jacket, and even upside down recognised the genre which public libraries put in shelves marked 'Romance'—a wild-haired woman with improbably large eyes and pointed chin, a rearing horse, quasi-Regency clothes, and a landscape in the background.

A tape on the woman's overall labelled her as Mrs Roberts. She turned the book politely to face the man as she handed it to him, and said, 'I don't honestly think—of course, I don't know everything outside Halemouth. I'll have a look—there's the National Trust Guide, and the National Gardens Scheme. I'll see if I can find anything.' She began to thumb through some of her brochures. 'What do you think you'd call it? A monument? Or a folly?'

Lindsay went down the town hall's steps. It had begun

to rain. A man went by bearing an announcement about the end of the world on sandwich boards which he was tilting to try to protect his hair from the shower. A tourist bus with its top deck open to the air drove slowly along the road, occupied only by two dejected Asians with fingers on their camera buttons. Lindsay scuttled across the road to The Copper Kettle. It was full of women who made Lindsay begin to understand why Venetia needed to wear the uniform.

The man who had been in the Town Hall came in as Lindsay sat down, and stood looking round the café: a middle-aged man wearing clothes he probably thought made him look younger, with hair sparsely sprouting on his pink chin and upper lip. He crossed the room to Lindsay's table.

'May I?'

'I suppose so.' The waitress came nearer.

'There's a vacant table upstairs,' she said.

'Thanks, but I'm fine here.' They each ordered coffee. Lindsay opened the town guide and read about a new sewerage scheme and the county's plans for a multi-million-pound sports centre. She could feel that the man was staring at her. She stirred her coffee without looking up. He said, 'You look exactly like a friend of mine.' She made an uninterested sound, and turned the page to find a list of the names and addresses of all the district and parish councillors. 'I thought when I first caught sight of you, over there, I thought that you were her. Now I can see the difference, but at first glance—well. My name's Mike Roper.'

'Oh. Hullo.' Lindsay pushed the town guide aside and waved to the waitress that she wanted more coffee. She looked around the room at the watercolours of the estuary and other local beauty spots, all labelled with the name of the painter and an optimistic price. The other customers were eating, with arch protestations, cream cakes and biscuits. Mike Roper was staring at her, almost avidly.

Lindsay sighed. She said, 'You're not my type. Sorry, and all that.'

'I'm not making a pass, honestly. It's just that you're so like Jane. I'm sure you must know her.'

'Not that I know of.'

'She wrote this book, actually.' He pulled it out again from the briefcase. Lindsay held the volume in her hands, amused at the picture on the cover, which reminded her of the escape literature she had enjoyed as a teenager. She glanced at the page where it fell open, and read a few lines, and her eyebrows lifted into a high arch. She tried at random some other passages in the book, her amusement growing, and in a moment she leant back and laughed, so heartily and naturally that she felt quite kindly towards the man who had provided such a source of pleasure.

'It's absolutely superb,' she gasped at last. 'What a marvellous book.'

'I didn't think it was all that funny,' he said.

'Didn't you? I haven't laughed so much for months. What a giveaway! Who is the author? Does it say anything about her? Oh, Jane Shore, I see.'

She started reading at page one. The opening of the book, in a stately home, full of lords and ladies addressing one another as such, did not seem much different from other historical romances she had read. It was as though the writer had swallowed the Regency legend whole, the dashing dandies with hearts of gold, the delicate damsels, the languishing ladies, without, of course, any but the most cursory mention of the lower classes, and then only in the capacity of loyal servants, impeccably trained. How selectively the writers of these fantasies researched, she thought. And would their heirs of the twenty-second century write only about dashing footballers and racing-car drivers, long-legged girls whose freedom was only skin deep and admiring proletarians living contented lives in their garden suburbs? I'll show them, she thought; though if they ignore Mayhew and Hogarth, what hope for Lindsay Fell?

'I should like to read this properly,' she said.

'Do borrow it. I've got two copies.'

'Well, thanks, but—'

'I thought of staying at the hotel for a day or so, I've got some business here. What is it—The Crown and Anchor. You could drop it back to me there.'

'All right. I shouldn't think it will take very long to get through,' Linday said. In any case, she thought, I wouldn't want to be seen reading it at Senhouse.

'You—uh— Do you know the author?' Mike said.

'I don't think so,' Lindsay answered coldly. 'Why do you ask?'

'I just thought—she lives around here, for one thing.'

'In Halemouth?'

'Somewhere near it, I believe. In the country. That's why I asked about the pagoda on the cover picture, I thought it might be a real place she described in the book. Might have been a well-known beauty spot or monument.'

'Are you trying to find her or something? What are you —a private eye?'

'No, no. Just an admirer. Of the book, I mean.'

'Really. Couldn't the publishers have given you her address?'

'They didn't have it.'

'Then how did you get this far? What makes you think she lives round here at all?'

'Oh, well, the publishers knew that much, as a matter of fact.'

'Look her up,' Lindsay said. 'In the telephone book.'

'I did and she's not in it. There is only one family called Shore and I went there. They couldn't possibly be the ones.'

Lindsay stood up. 'Thanks for the loan.' She walked quickly from the café.

The rain had stopped and the centre of Halemouth was filling up; the car park flashed a red light to show that it was full, and there were queues in the bus station. Across the car park from the Town Hall was the public library, built to last, sober, dignified, a temple to self-improvement. Three years before, when Lindsay had gone to Halemouth to pick up something forgotten for a week-end house party, she had been asked to sign a petition to save it from demolition. It was surpassingly inconvenient to run and expensive to maintain; it had too little shelf space for its floor area and needed electric light on all day. But apparently anyone who had grown up in Hale-mouth regarded it as an essential feature of the townscape. The preservationists must have won, for now painters were at work on its windows and slaters repairing the roof.

Lindsay scuttled inside it before Mike could pay for the coffee and follow her. The reading-room was upstairs, and she sat down at a table beside a man who was working his way through a stack of every political weekly paper.

She was almost embarrassed to start reading. The action of opening the book did not feel illicit; Lindsay had a shared childhood's experience of reading Venetia's diaries and letters whenever the opportunity had offered. Her recent abstinence from exploring Venetia's open desk had not been from any adult sense of honour, but was caused merely by her lack of interest in Venetia's mono-gamous and rustic life. She hesitated now because the few words she had already read seemed so pathetic. It was as though Venetia had admitted a passion for a film star or a king, as though she had exposed a teenage immaturity behind her elder-sisterly façade in the hope of attracting sympathy without realising that the tears she provoked would be of laughter.

But perhaps she had just wanted to make some money. After all, it should be as safe a form of literature to boil a pot over as any.

There was no doubt in Lindsay's mind that Venetia Jane Sennen, daughter of Iris Fell, *née* Shore, had written the book; the name alone might not have proved it, but the idealised pagoda did. Lindsay had trudged around the damned thing often enough these last few weeks, she thought, to have its existence imprinted on her mind. Not that the reality was at all like this cover picture. As in the party game, where a whispered message is translated into something quite different by the time it reaches the end of a line of children, so the monument described in the book and drawn by a stranger from that description had altered; but a pagoda was a pagoda—and how many of those were there in Britain, connected with a woman whose name had once been Shore?

At Senhouse an artificial lake had been constructed where before the early nineteenth century had been a boggy field. Now water surrounded the hillock on which Hugh's ancestor had caused to be erected the largest of his trophies. The pagoda was shabby now, its surface dulled by time. The children had rubber dinghies on the lake, and would ferry visitors to the island; the arched bridge trembled at a footstep. Hugh kept sheep on the lawns, and the grass was short, but the shrubberies which used to frame the view were shaggy, and the bushes, unpruned, flowered sparsely. Around the lake there was a muddy path, along which Lindsay had set herself to walk like a cruise passenger on a ship's deck.

Lindsay read and thought that what she read was rubbish. At the same time, she was obliged to admit that she recognised with an almost guilty pleasure the emotions that light romantic literature provoked, the identification with an impossible heroine which had formed a welcome interruption to her homework in former years. She felt sad for her younger self, that she had needed such an escape, when the world had been so full of accessible but forbidden fulfilments, and sadder to realise that this book had been written for adults to read, by an adult whose own life was, to strangers' eyes, as full as any woman's could be.

It was the first of what Mike Roper had called the 'hot passages' which horrified Lindsay the most: not that she was shocked by their frankness, but that, reading them, she felt sure that they were derived entirely from imagination. Like the other adventures of the improbable heroine, the author was not writing what she knew about.

She could have asked me, Lindsay thought; and was wrung with pity that Venetia might have missed something which her younger sister knew so well.

She finished the book in less than two hours, and sat looking at its cover wondering what on earth to do about it. No wonder, for one thing, that it had been published under a false name. Venetia should have been justified in thinking herself quite safe from anyone who knew the names on her family tree having any sight of the book. Lindsay herself was not much of a reader at all, which had made her convalescence even more boring; Simon, in Glasgow, read only travel books. Although he had never shown any signs of regretting his staid insularity, Lindsay deduced a lot from his bookshelves. Iris Fell used to have books chosen for her regularly by the librarians at Harrods. But she rarely read the books—biographies, mostly—before they were due to be returned.

No, if it had not been for the accident of Lindsay's having been at Halemouth's Information Bureau at the same time as the man who called himself Mike, Venetia would have been safe from discovery ... what bad luck. It was no wonder, after all, that Venetia should not have wished to be known as the author of *A Pleasure to Come*. Her neighbours would think it revealed her private life; her sister realised something she might have wished known even less: that it gave away only her private fantasies.

But who, and this was the urgent question, was Mike? It seemed utterly implausible that he should merely be a reader trying to seek out his dream book's writer. Such things were the products of minds like the one which had invented the dramas of Babs Gwynn, not of the life of the nineteen seventies. But if not that, then what?

A middle-aged man, in Lindsay's mind an 'older man', Hugh's age perhaps; wishing to be thought younger and smarter than he was; sexy, in his own way, with those hot blue eyes, though unattractively pink skinned and rounded on all surfaces like stomach, cheeks, nose and eyeballs; professional, or at least a salary rather than a wage earner, but hard to visualise in a City of London uniform; there was no reason to suppose that Mike was not his name. What could he possibly want with Venetia? Or rather, with Jane Shore? It might, Lindsay thought, be quite fun to find out.

On the other hand, there was no doubt that the last thing Venetia would want was for him to find her.

Lindsay gathered her fringed leather bag, the new basket she had bought that morning, her coat and her shawl, and went out into a Halemouth now glistening and improved by sunshine. She was tempted to keep the copy of the book, but decided against it, in case Venetia noticed it in her room before Lindsay had decided what, if anything, she was going to say. The Crown and Anchor was up the hill from the library, and though Lindsay disliked alcohol, she was pleased to see that it was not quite closing time.

She went into the public bar and ordered herself some tonic water and the only remaining sandwich, a sagging pillow of sliced eggs in white bread. It did not worry her that she hardly fitted in with the other users of the hotel, a few drinkers in tweeds stoking up until the evening and a hard-faced woman in sheepskin. She had learnt to ignore standing out from a crowd, having as a child disliked and as a teenager revelled in it.

I'll catch the bus at half past two, she thought. I can get away without him knowing anything about where I come from. But as she went towards the desk, where she intended to ask the receptionist to take the book, he came up to her.

'I am told there's a handsome row of almshouses here. Would you like to come and see it with me?'

'Almshouses!' Lindsay exclaimed.

'I know.' He became pinker still. 'Well, I'm not really all that interested either. To be perfectly frank with you, I wanted to talk to you.' Lindsay found herself walking along the road towards Halemouth's ancient church and almshouses listening to Mike. 'I dare say you have been wondering what I want with Jane Shore,' he said, and Lindsay prepared herself to hear a lie. 'I'll be honest, it sounds peculiar. Embarrassing even. I met her in London, at a party. A publisher's party. I write children's books, sort of educational ones. She was wearing a belt, and my wife fell in love with it. She's like that, Christine is, I mean. Well, she asked, and Jane Shore told her what it was, some modern silversmith made it. Now the fact is my wife's been going on about it ever since, she wants a belt like that, why can't I get her one. Well, I can't for the life of me remember the name of the chap that made it. Christine didn't hear it in the first place, and I've got a memory like a sieve. Well, you know how it is, there's only one thing for it in the end, I said I'd try to find Jane

Shore and ask her again. I expect you think I'm hen-pecked,' he said with an unconvincing laugh. 'I'd not contradict you. Though I'll be honest with you, it was a lovely bit of stuff. Silver links, with bits of carving and some white stones in it.' Lindsay did not say anything; he was describing a moonstone and silver belt that she had brought Venetia from Israel a few years before when it looked as though waists were going to be worn again. 'I must say,' he went on, 'when I set eyes on you in the town hall, I thought for a moment—well, you do have a look of her, you know. Do you happen to know her, actually?'

'I don't know anyone of that name,' Lindsay said.

'It's probably not her full name. You live round here, don't you? I thought that pagoda in the story was probably a real place, it's the sort of thing that does exist. There's one at Kew Gardens. I shouldn't be surprised to find she lives somewhere near a place like that, if there is one near Halemouth. I'm a bit disappointed actually, I thought there might be one here, in a park or something, like a bandstand. But there isn't.'

'I must go,' Lindsay said. 'I am sorry I can't help you. I think the best thing you could do would be to go back to London, if that's where you come from. You could ask at the Craft Centre about silversmiths.'

'You don't like me, do you?' he said, smiling a little. 'I think you could help me if you wanted to. Is Jane Shore a relation of yours really? I'm a lawyer, as a matter of fact, I'm used to weighing up witnesses. Are you telling me the truth?'

'Why should I answer that?'

'Well, I'll tell you one thing. You may not like me, but she did! Just bear that in mind when you decide what to tell me. She certainly did.'

Lindsay walked away rapidly to the bus station. She glanced around when she got there, but he was too far behind her to see which bus she got into of a row of four, and she bent forward as it drew out of the station so that he would not be able to see her through the window.

So her sister had liked the little man, had she? She watched unnoticing as the bus took her through the wooded roads, and wondered what he meant by that. She would have been surprised and dismayed to hear what Mike was saying.

He was talking to the porter in the Crown and Anchor.

'Did you see the young lady who left that book for me?'

'Yes, I did.'

'Did you know her, by any chance?'

'Yes, I have seen her, I don't know her name, but she comes in with Mr and Mrs Sennen sometimes.'

'Mrs Sennen?'

'Yes, everyone knows them round here, they live at Senhouse. About five miles away. Quite a showpiece it used to be in the old days, they say.' Mike was no longer listening. He was thinking triumphantly of the way people knew what was going on in the country. He'd thought it would be like that. There would be no anonymity for Mrs Sennen or her sister in a place this size; so much the better for him.

PART THREE

'A Day in the Life of Venetia Sennen.' She thought of the title as she glanced at the open page of the family diary for the next day: 'Harriet dentist, 9; lunch Fiona, to discuss arrangements for the NSPCC ball; village fête, Red Cross 7.'

'What a pillar of the community I seem to be,' she said aloud.

'What?' Hugh came into the hall from the library, carrying two decanters on a slightly tarnished tray. 'Can you order some more Madeira, Venetia?'

'All right. But it's gone up again.'

'Better get a dozen, before it goes up further still.'

'Listen to my day tomorrow.' She read aloud the list of her engagements.

'You are good, darling. You do a wonderful job,' he said. He padded into the pantry, a long cubicle now only used for the machine which made fizzy drinks and for Hugh's own silver-cleaning materials. He would not do the knives and forks but was prepared to polish the pieces of silver which Venetia would otherwise have put away wrapped in baize and polythene. He insisted on using his grandfather's epergne and the salver which lay on the hall table, even though the only cards now deposited on it bore the names of representatives of firms selling animal foods and farm machinery.

It was raining and Venetia went into the drawing-room to close the windows. Lindsay had already gone to bed when Venetia came in from her parent-teachers' association meeting and her bedroom light was out, though the light in the bathroom had been left on, and Venetia had found the bath full of scummy water and all the towels water-logged on the floor. The mirror had been decorated with toothpaste patterns, but Venetia was too tired to clean it.

The drawing-room at least was in perfect order, for Venetia had not had time to go in it all day and Lindsay had been out. The children had been having a bending race on their tricycles between the room and the veranda, in and out of the open french doors. It was perfectly safe, as the pillars of the balustrade were close together, but Hugh disapproved of the game, and was prone to remark, 'Isn't there a nursery in this house?' Venetia said that houses were for people to live in and she had moved the spindle-leg tables and the Chinese carpet to the other side of the room. She noticed a small tear in the wallpaper beside one of the windows. The paper had been brought back from China and hung in the room a century before. She adjusted the heavy, faded curtain to cover the tear and thought that with any luck Hugh would never notice it.

Venetia was tired, but keyed up, after a rather acri-monious meeting in which irreconcilable differences of opinion about school uniform had been repeated many times by parents and teachers. If she went straight to bed she would spend the night reliving the irritations she had suppressed when their objects were there, and re-phrasing the cutting remarks she might have made. She lit a cigarette and sat on the seat in the bay window which Hugh's grandmother had caused to be made on the garden side of the room. Such embellishments would have been regarded as vandalism now. The house was a listed building and subject to innumerable planning controls. It consisted of the original house on to which an eighteenth-century front had been built at right angles, doubling the number of rooms and turning a farmer's home into a gentleman's residence. Hugh had often complained that the twentieth-century reverence for the architectural standards of the past was illogical. He ought to be allowed, if he could afford it, to build on an extension which would be admired two centuries hence. But his frustration was only on principle; he would not have altered a square inch of Senhouse.

A heavy scent of jasmine came into the room through the open sash window. In the winter the prevailing winds blew draughts into all the rooms at the front of the house and the family tended to huddle into the back sitting-room as close as they could get to the log fire. But the drawing-room was attractive in summer, with Virginia creeper and wisteria over the veranda and a flower bed planted with sweet-smelling herbaceous flowers under the west window. Some years one could lean out and pluck a nectarine from the tree which grew against the wall. Venetia could imagine how her children would enjoy, when they were adolescents, sitting on the window seat and reading poetry, with occasional glances at the evocative views of the flowers, garden and lawn, and the cornfields, and avenue of trees leading to the lake. Or perhaps not poetry: sensitive novels about growing up; or Henry James. There should be the tapping of croquet mallets and tennis racquets in the distance. She would ask Hugh to bring the croquet box down from the store above the potting shed.

There were Hugh's footsteps overhead now; he always went to bed before Venetia, and he thought she was un-friendly if she sat up reading. She got up and plumped the sofa cushions. Like everything else in the room, it showed its age, but it would be hard to find another velvet which looked like the ghost of its original colour; this room, and in fact most of the house, had a charm and a dignity which came from having been virtually unchanged for generations. Venetia felt that if she improved anything it would make everything else suddenly ridiculous. Not, she thought, as she went through the house checking on the locks, that it was as she would have chosen. Hugh had left the side door from the library open, and she pulled it to, and slid the bolt across. The library, she thought, pausing by the door with her hand on the light switch, expressed what she knew of Hugh's personality almost uncannily well, considering that he had neither added to nor subtracted from the furniture when it became his. But that was partly the point; he had a complete reverence for tradition and his family's past, which made this room ideally suited to him. The room was a long, low rectangle, which had once been two rooms in the smaller house. It was lined with glass-fronted bookcases, and in the gaps between them hung portraits of Hugh's ancestors: a Sennen in green drab, by Opie, a Sargent of the one who was killed in the First World War, a wonderful realisation of Hugh's mother by Gwen John.

The desk was large and flat-topped, and the tattered leather was concealed by maps spread under glass sheets. Hugh kept his papers in order and only used the room for his private life. All the farm work was done in the little office which had once been the dairy, when the cows still came into the part of the yard where now they kept the cars and hung the washing.

There was a picture postcard on the mantelpiece of a Grecian temple above a brilliant sea: from Ann, lucky Ann. Venetia turned it over to read the commonplaces to which her mother-in-law restricted her correspondence. 'Wonderful weather, scenery even better. Can't think why I never came before. Do remember to sort out the cabinets for Dorothy Westbourne. She writes that she wants to bring a friend from the British Museum. Love to all, A.'

Venetia let the card drop out of her hand into the hearth. She bent and scratched on the smooth marble to pick it up, and replaced it where Hugh had left it, leaning against a watercolour miniature of his adventurous grandmother in her pre-flying days. Venetia wondered what she would have done in the circumstances.

She straightened the fire irons and mopped at a patch of wood ash on the carpet with her handkerchief. She went into the kitchen to check the door and the taps. The water supply was uncertain enough without letting it drip uselessly all night. The dog grunted and whined in the back kitchen. He wanted to start the day all over again. But he was out of favour, having brought in a moribund rabbit after lunch and added it to the pile of french beans which Venetia was stringing before they could be blanched and frozen.

Up the stairs Henry and Harriet were asleep in characteristic positions, Harriet with her nose in the air and her bedclothes hardly disturbed, Henry as though he fought enemies in his dreams. Venetia picked up his shirt and trousers and hung them on the chair. There was a rim of dirt round the shirt collar and the trousers were beginning to split at the crutch again. The headmaster had said, at the meeting that evening, that the boys would attend school without collars and ties over his head body.

Hugh was already asleep and snoring. He looked incongruously humdrum with his weather-toughened face and balding head in the pretty four-poster bed. The green muslin curtain swelled in and out, as if in time with his breathing, in the draught.

Venetia sat down at her dressing-table, a beautiful piece of furniture on which ivory-backed brushes and cut-glass jars were arranged. From the drawer she took her plastic hair brush and cheap face cream in a tube. This room represented the achievement of a minor ambition. When she was about sixteen and as silly a teenager as she could possibly fear Harriet might become, she had seen her vision of the perfect lady's bedroom in a stately home which she had visited with a school party. She hardly remembered the rest of the house, the art treasures and architectural niceties merged with many others in her mind. But she had always remembered and been determined to reproduce the bedroom, with its chintz and frills and silver-framed photographs, and an air of luxury and indolence which, she found, demanded hardish labour to keep up.

The bed had been in one of the spare bedrooms when Hugh and Venetia moved into the house. Ann had insisted, as enlightened brides did in her day, on twin divans from Heals. But all the previous Mrs Sennens had slept between these four posts of entwined yew wood: Hugh's grandmother, the adventurous Lady Edith Sennen, his short-lived great-grandmother, Dorothy, and before her Harriet and Amelia and Elizabeth, each with her respective Henry or Hugh.

The mattress was new, at least; Venetia lay on her back with her knees drawn up, to press the aching base of her spine against its hardness. Hugh grunted, and turned away on his side, hunching the bedclothes over his face. He exuded warmth, though he was on the far side of the wide bed. And with the physical comfort had always in the past come the certainty of his dependability and permanence, security in his trust and affection. Venetia had never doubted him. She was sure it had never occurred to him to doubt her.

Hugh had represented a romantic ideal when Venetia met him, the product of a rural stability which her upbringing had taught her provided the perfect way of life. He was handsome, self-confident and knew where he was going, doubting his future as little as he queried his roots.

The first Sennen remembered by his descendants had been a ship's boy risen to captain during the Napoleonic wars. Prize money had first bought and later enlarged the farmhouse, whose name had been changed to Senhouse at the same time as the family applied for and, after considerable payment, was granted a coat of arms. The real wealth had been acquired later in the century by a seafaring ancestor who chose the merchant navy, and brought home loot from the Far East. Hugh's father had been the first of the family to farm the land himself, having had enough of the sea on Atlantic convoys. Hugh read agriculture at Cambridge and continued to toy with academic forestry; he published terse articles about the diseases of trees. He was not, as Venetia sometimes found herself defensively thinking, by any means a Philistine, indeed he was very knowledgeable about the furniture and pictures and objets d'art he had inherited, though whether he had taken the trouble to learn about them the better to indulge his ancestor worship was something Venetia preferred not to wonder. Whatever his motives, Hugh could identify antiques as easily as he could distinguish types of tree or cow, and though he did not or perhaps could not add to them he valued his belongings for more than their money's worth.

He valued his family too. Venetia knew that perfectly well, she had not the slightest doubt that Hugh had mapped out a path for his emotions when they married and would not dream of straying off it. He would never think of wondering whether he still loved his wife, but would assume their mutual affection until the day he died —unless some inescapable contradiction was presented to him.

Venetia turned restlessly, and curled herself into a foetal

119

position. How could she make any convincing answer to the question he, or Lindsay, or even someone else might be asking her? She knew well enough herself, but the truth, she felt, was neither plausible nor exculpatory. For she had never admitted even to Hugh that his lovemaking had left her disappointed.

That was the basis of all that she had done. She could know it, unspoken, her face pressed into her crossed arms, in the silence and dark of the curtained bed. But in an age of physical freedoms even the thought, let alone the voicing of it, was one which she pushed away, could hardly refine into words. So long as her awareness was not reduced into the code which communicated it, she could deny it to herself, as she had done, for years. Indeed, before the frankness of a new generation had splashed on to her consciousness descriptions of unknown experiences, she was not sure that she was missing anything. She had not read the French editions of manuals and novels which her more daring contemporaries smuggled into Britain.

Her sexual instruction had consisted of her mother's hasty excuse that she was sure that Venetia already knew all there was to know; of the giggled imprecisions and evasions that her generation of girls had whispered to each other; of the clinical bullying she had experienced at a session with a woman gynaecologist just before her marriage, who had scorned her patients' clumsiness with her appliances, and stood over them coldly watching, while they tried to insert the intractable rubber. Hugh had taught her the mechanics of actions with which she found she could express love but not passion. But he was satisfied; and so was she, until she began to read in literature newly available what she was missing.

It might have been possible to discuss it with Hugh at the very beginning of their marriage. Five years later she knew better than to imply the criticism. Her own inhibitions were matched by his; and her tentative experiments in variety were more embarrassing than enjoyable. There were still physical privacies between husband and wife.

Venetia had read sexy books and magazines and been absorbed in them in an almost academic way, for the gymnastics, sensations and photographed bodies seemed outside any experience she might ever have. But gradually her imagination grew on what it fed on; it was in this bed, in this secret curled position, that she had reverted to her childhood satisfaction of fantasied adventure. The story of Lady Babs Gwynn had begun as the secret saga of Venetia Sennen. Writing it down in the form of a provincial lady describing her grandmother's exploits had freed her mind of what was beginning to obsess it.

Hugh sat up suddenly. 'You're awake, aren't you?'

'Mm.' Venetia stretched her cramped limbs into an appearance of relaxation. Hugh had an uncanny trick of seeming to be woken by the sound of her mind working. He lay down closer to her and drew her into his arms, stroking her shoulders.

'Take it off,' he said, pulling at her nightdress. Venetia turned to him ardently. Mike's assuaging of her physical restlessness bore no relationship to the demonstration of unity that she wanted to give her husband.

It was not even as though she liked the man, after all. A few months later she could hardly believe in the impulse which had taken her even to that first dinner with him, let alone into his dirty bed.

Venetia had sent her manuscript to Palfrey & Blackwood merely, in a way, because it was there—fifty thousand consecutive words which she had enjoyed scribbling and found amusing to re-read. She had used a concocted name and given the return address of a post office in Central London. It had only become necessary to concoct a more plausible-seeming existence for the people who knew her as Jane Shore when she discovered, to her own amazement, that the book would be published, and that Palfrey & Blackwood even had hopes of American and paperback sales. The possibility of success made it even more important to preserve her pseudonimity. Venetia had not been able to decide whether it would be worse for Hugh to be shown her lecherous imagination, or for her neighbours to conclude that her experience was wanton. But there seemed no reason why Jane Shore should ever be revealed as Venetia Sennen. She had been sure that her tracks were untraceably covered.

Indeed, it had not been Venetia Sennen who stood in that room at the Palfrey & Blackwood party, but another personality, a woman who was free from the knowledge that others expected any particular actions or behaviour of her, who would not be judged as anyone's mother or wife but who might present any image she chose to the world. And the image she had chosen was different indeed from that of the worthy provincial lady.

Jane Shore had put herself into the hands of a hair artist and a visagiste, knowing from past experience that her appearance always reverted to its natural state before a long evening was over, like Cinderella's. She had bought a dress which she knew would not be useful in her normal life, and as she drew its folds over the curled hair, felt herself putting on with it the freedom of disguise; it was what people must have felt at masked balls.

So it was not Venetia who had accepted Mike Roper's dinner invitation. She would have thought him common and comic; but she would not have been likely ever to meet him. To Jane Shore he appeared entertaining. She was titillated by the glint in his eye. She was liberated by anonymity.

But I'm not a fool, Venetia thought, as she caressed

Hugh's back and returned his kisses. She knew perfectly well that Mike was no demon lover, it wasn't his skill compared with ineptness on Hugh's part which galvanised her in bed with him. It was the releasing of inhibitions— knowing that there was nobody to hear, and if there were, nobody to recognise; that nothing more would be read into her intimate actions than a sensual urge, and that she was not implying any other involvement. Every gesture she made with Hugh, she thought, as she touched the parts of his body she knew he liked to have touched, bore messages with it, of knowledge, and consideration, and their shared experience. Jane Shore was a woman newly born, who had sprung fully armed in self-confidence and sensuality from the head of her inventor.

Hugh settled himself to sleep again, his hand on her thigh. She lay still for a moment, and then pushed herself off the bed. She could not sleep naked now that the children were of an age to come into their parents' bedroom. She decided to have a bath in the hope of making herself feel like sleep. The water was soft and discoloured, untreated by chemicals. She poured some green crystals into the tub, and watched them dissolve; scented steam rose into her face. Her body felt healed and soothed in the almost too sharp heat. She lowered herself gently into the water, watched the tide of red on her skin. Hugh had given her the fresh lemony bath salts. He gave his mother musky French scent. She wondered if that was obscurely meaningful. The real question was not why she had gone with Mike that first time; anyone could be excused a single impulse. But to have returned again and again, inventing reasons for going away from home—that was the real unfaithfulness.

Yet even now, glancing dispassionately at her own body in the water, she remembered the release, the abandon of Venetia's restraint when Jane relaxed in nakedness. Jane

123

had not cared whether her skin was slackening or her
figure thickening, for there was no younger perfection for
its watcher to remember; she had not held back her
gestures or attitudes in the fear of what they might imply.
Venetia was unable to slacken her guard, even with Hugh.
Jane, with Mike, could be shameless. The freedom must
have been similar to what Lindsay got from her drugs.
Anonymity, Venetia thought, was the best narcotic.

The bath was cooling, and there would be no more hot
water until the morning. Venetia heaved herself out and
sat wrapped in the towel on the side of the bath, sniffing
the scented warmth that rose from her skin. What did
other people think was under the façade of Mrs Sennen?
She wondered whether they saw her as an individual, or
as the representative of a class and type—the next generation at Senhouse. Even the friends she and Hugh saw—
not as often as they would like, what with the evening
meetings, the dawn milkings and the other incidents of
their lives—those friends· thought of her as Hugh's wife
doing a good job. It hadn't been inevitable. Venetia could
have made the choice not to get involved in the work she
did, and to have concentrated more on herself, inspiring
glints in the eyes of other women's husbands, and emitting
messages of availability.

She laughed a little to think of that phrase. Availability
must be signalled unconsciously too. The first time that
a man other than Hugh had looked at her in a sexual
way since her marriage had been at a party not long ago.
Godfrey Pugh, the husband of one of Venetia's best
friends, had suddenly started his spiel after knowing her
for nine years and never so much as playing footsy before.
He was very attractive, much more so than Mike Roper.
But Venetia would have died sooner than have him see
her undressed.

But I'm only thirty-three, she thought, two children

and a nursery diet haven't turned me into a hag. If I were not married I'd count as a girl and flaunt a bikini. Shan't I have any more affairs?

She knew the answer to that. She was as old as she felt, and she felt middle-aged. Jane Shore died young.

In spite of going to sleep so late Venetia woke when Hugh got up to do the milking. A light mist was lingering at ground level, but above it was blue sky and the smell of a perfect day. Venetia got up to enjoy it while she could, wishing that she had no list of duties for the day. She went out to see how her garden grew. Her bare feet slid about in the sandals as the dew wet them; it was still chilly, but it would be sunny for the fête. Venetia reminded herself to iron the dress she had planned to wear if it was fine.

The day went according to the plan made for it. Harriet cried in the dentist and had to be persuaded to enter her school when it was already break time; lunch with Fiona was delicious and predictable, and Fiona talked, as always, about dogs. It was funny, Venetia thought, as she made the prescribed responses to both events, how it was necessary to say the words. After all, Harriet knew that she would cry and her mother would comfort her, that she would try to get out of going back to school and that she would be induced to do it. Fiona, Venetia, and the other women at lunch could all have predicted the very sentences they spoke at lunch, yet they had to go through with it. Would it feel the same at the end of the day if the whole lot had taken place in imagination only? Venetia often found that she could not remember whether something had really happened, and occasionally wondered if it made any difference. Sometimes she had washed, dressed, breakfasted and walked the dog, only to wake in bed and find that she had done her duties only in her mind. Still, she reminded herself, the cavities in Harriet's teeth were objective.

The fête had been timed so that the children coming out of school and their mothers could look in to the vicarage garden and spend their money without any special effort. Venetia gave Harriet and Henry something to spend and begged them to go away with it, as it embarrassed her to have them listen to her speeches, but they stood near the platform (an upturned trailer) and Harriet was evidently hoping that she would be pointed out as the Opener's daughter; she tugged at her hair ribbon and simpered, and smoothed the skirt of her Liberty print dress. Venetia knew that she would be comparing it unfavourably with Sharon Webb's pink frills and the two-piece bathing suit with which Carol James's skinny, sexless, eight-year-old body had been clothed.

Miss Trevail was making little stacks of change on the edge of her stall; she knew that her punnets of strawberries would be sold out in five minutes of the fête being declared open. The ground behind her was already piled with the fruit reserved by her favoured customers. Mrs Oliver, the vicar's wife, stood beside Venetia, but her eyes were anxiously on the table where she had displayed a year's worth of knitting and stitching. The wrong time of year to sell soft toys, she had murmured, and Venetia had been obliged to assure her that she at least was glad of the opportunity to buy Christmas presents well in advance. Old Dumpy Amis waited on no speeches but briskly scooped and smoothed ice cream for the queueing children.

From the vicarage garden could be seen glimpses of the street through the hedge and of graves through the belt of elm trees. On one side the church tower, much admired by Pevsner, on the other the comfortable neatness of the red-brick vicarage, with its windows hospitably open on to the garden, framed the traditional scene. Fêtes in the vicarage garden must have been the same for a hundred years, Venetia thought, except that she, on her platform, was just 'that Mrs Sennen', and the amount of small change she would be expected to disperse would make a noticeable hole in her budget. In a community the size of this one, she would not even be able to present to the next fête the purchases she made at this. When she died her executors would find a cupboard at Senhouse bulging with knitted animals in vibrant colours, doilies, tea cosies, artificial flowers and Christmas decorations. She hoped something worth having would be left by the time she reached the stalls; she would actually be glad to buy home-made cake and strawberries.

Venetia pulled uneasily at her dress, which seemed to have shrunk since the last time she had worn it, and hoped that the belt buckle would hide the fact that the hook and eye at the waist had burst.

Canon Oliver cleared his throat thunderously, and finding himself ignored, rang the dinner bell which his wife handed him. Reluctantly most of the people in his garden turned towards the platform. He introduced Venetia by saying that she needed no introduction, and then made the speech which he had delivered unaltered every year since he came to the parish. Venetia smiled generally around, and glanced at her watch. The best piece of advice that she had been given by her mother-in-law was never to speak for more than two minutes on such occasions. She could see that Tracy James was clutching a bunch of orange roses shrouded in 'polythene, with which she would presumably be presented, and wondered, as the vicar reached his familiar peroration, whether to make some graceful allusion to the fact that the flowers were golden and that this must be the fiftieth fête she had opened in the locality since marrying Hugh. But she decided that the remark might be tactless; and the idea was driven from her mind as she stepped forward in response to the vicar's gesture. For as she glanced around the garden, and opened her mouth, she saw at the back of the small crowd a face which drove all words from her tongue and all thoughts from her mind.

'Venetia, are you all right?' Mrs Oliver whispered urgently.

'What? Oh—yes, sorry.' She launched automatically into the words which she had practised, complete with all the necessary compliments and thanks. She did not think she had said anything disastrous; nobody had a more interested or shocked expression than was usual, except for that one. She avoided looking at him again. Mrs Oliver was thanking her. Tracy James was staggering up to her with the orange roses. Thank Tracy James. Thank Mrs Oliver silently with a convincing-looking smile. Smile at the crowd. Listen to Canon Oliver thanking the deity. Realise that sooner or later she would have to descend from the relative impregnability of the platform into danger.

Miss Kershaw, the children's teacher, was waiting to tell her about the swimming-pool appeal fund. Hugh had promised to provide the tractor and the work of some of his men once enough money had been raised, and Miss Kershaw wanted her to rejoice that the target had nearly been reached, and that the Webb children's father had offered the loan of some earth-moving equipment. Venetia found herself promising to organise a fund-raising donkey Derby at Senhouse.

The strawberries were all sold. The only cakes left were rich fruit or coffee, both much disliked by the children: buy one and remember to take it to old Miss Carew in hospital on Monday. Henry wanted some more money. Harriet wanted her to buy a doll dressed like a Spanish dancer made by Miss Kershaw. The bottle stall: she bought two tickets and won one small pot of horseradish sauce. The Lucky Dip: Henry found a plastic pair of scissors and Harriet a small china mouse which she promptly dropped and broke. Venetia gave her another ten pence and sent the children off to get more ice creams. Mr Simmonds's secondhand book stall, with the same volumes, smelling even damper, that he had offered last year. Venetia bought back what had once been her own volume of nineteenth-century verse. Mr Simmonds wanted to talk about the new sewerage scheme, and she had to listen to all he had to say although he had agreed that it would be better addressed to Hugh. The jumble stall, with the usual depressing sight of mothers fighting over miserable discarded garments; it was not even, as Mrs Oliver whispered, as though they all looked as though they needed to.

Venetia put her dark glasses on and pulled her straw trilby further down over her face. She glanced warily around. He did not seem to be nearby.

'I mustn't stay too late,' she said.

'Oh my dear, you can't go,' Mrs Oliver protested. 'Such a lovely day, we're so lucky for the Brownies' display. You must stay for the concert.' Venetia had forgotten the concert. She would not be forgiven if she left before it.

'I've got a meeting tonight,' she said weakly.

'So have I, the Red Cross isn't it? I suppose they couldn't manage without us? No, that's a naughty thought, isn't it?' Mrs Oliver said, twinkling matily at Venetia. 'Never mind, Timothy and Hugh will just have to be grass widowers this evening again. And I'm sure your sister will put the children to bed for you.'

The tea tent: a gust of hot air came through the gap in the canvas. I don't want to be cornered in there, Venetia thought. She stood by the entrance, blocking her nose against the smell of hot mud and hot people. There was a queue for cups of tea. She couldn't hear herself think. Think: where was he? What was he doing here?

Mrs Oliver took her by the arm. 'Come along, my dear, Timothy has a table for us.'

'I don't think I—'

'My dear, I insist. You look quite pale. I was quite worried about you on the rostrum earlier on. A cup of tea will do you a world of good.'

A table made of fawn-coloured Formica; plastic chairs whose metal legs sank into the ground, orange, bitter tea. Venetia sipped and burnt her mouth. She was surrounded by stout women, most of whom she knew at least by sight. They were talking about the weather and the coming concert. They were getting up. The vicar had announced that the concert would start in five minutes. Outside into the sunlight, spotted now by the shadow of leaves as the sun sank below the treetops. Queues for the Portaloos. Mrs Oliver took her into the house and offered her the use of the bathroom.

The vicarage was cool inside, shabby and threadbare and under-used, a big house without a family to fill it. She sat in the bathroom, unchanged for years—a wooden lavatory seat with the varnish flaked off leaving paler stripes; a white bath stained with green patches, its claw-shaped feet standing on the floorboards where the red linoleum had not reached; thin striped towels and a smell of disinfectant, and of unluxurious soap.

'Are you all right, my dear?' Mrs Oliver's voice at the door.

'Yes, thank you so much. Here I am.'

Safe with the vicar's wife's arm through hers; the garden empty now, some stragglers outside in the village street, making towards the school; a few backs of people not duty bound to watch their children cavorting. Venetia peered

130

cautiously around. Over there, the back of a head—! She pulled Mrs Oliver's arm. 'We'll be late.' Looking straight ahead, she and Mrs Oliver scampered with an ungainly, adult, half-run half-walk towards the school. Was he following? She couldn't be sure, in one swift look before going in. Miss Kershaw had seen that seats were saved for the Olivers near the front, as the vicar was a school manager. Once in here Venetia was just a parent. She climbed over some knees to a vacant chair in the middle of the audience, and collapsed, safely surrounded by other mothers and fathers, on a chair built for a person not older than eleven. The vicar jumped on to the platform, and prayed. Miss Kershaw climbed the stairs to the platform and announced the programme. Thirty tots filed into view from behind a curtain. They sank a song about a dog and a banana. There were several solo performances on the violin; Harriet appeared in a group of children playing the recorder; Henry tried to hide in the back row of his class's rendering of the story of Noah's Flood. Some small girls in tutus came on to dance

Venetia looked at her neighbours. They all seemed pleased and entertained and still applauded everything fervently. It was already half past six, and Venetia realised that she would not be able to get to her evening meeting. Now some of the larger children were going to perform a play they had written themselves. Venetia clasped her hands very tightly. There seemed to be no reason why this display should ever come to an end. Perhaps it wasn't going to end, it would be like the story of the traveller on the London Underground who realised that the train would never stop. The familiar surroundings of amateur or childish performances, experienced so often by Venetia these last few years, would become her eternity. What am I doing, she thought, sitting in discomfort watching other people's children incompetently disporting themselves? How did I get landed with this?

The recorder group struck up the National Anthem, and the vicar said another prayer. Henry and Harriet pushed their way towards Venetia, shouting, 'Did you like it, Mummy? Was I good?'

'Run ahead to the car,' Venetia told them. 'Go on, I'm in a hurry.'

She stood at the school's door and measured the dash to her car with her eyes. She couldn't actually see him lying in wait for her. She set off briskly between two noisy family groups.

He was beside her. He gripped her arm. 'I must talk to you,' he said.

Someone will notice, she thought. He must have been in that gateway. Will they hear if I—? She stepped on to the verge, letting the people behind her walk on. Nobody would know that he wasn't just another child's father. Perhaps he even had been in the concert audience. 'What are you doing here?' she muttered.

'Looking for you. Where can we talk?'

'Nowhere. Not here. Please go away.'

'I'll come back if I do. I've been searching—you've no idea. Just to see you again—'

'I haven't anything to say to you,' she said fiercely. Mrs Oliver came towards them. She would wonder who he was, be surprised that there could be a father of a child at the village school she'd never seen. 'Too late for the Red Cross meeting, I'm afraid,' Venetia called.

'I know, you must get the children to bed. I'll look in and present your apologies, shall I?'

'Thanks, that's very good of you. Goodnight.' She had gone on. There were still some stragglers down the road. Henry called out of the car's window, 'I thought you were in a hurry, Mum?'

'Coming.' She turned back to Mike Roper. 'I don't know what the hell you are doing here. I don't want to see you, can't you understand that?'

'No, I don't believe you. You can't have changed so much. Tell me where you can meet me.'

'Nowhere. It's impossible.'

'I'll come to your house.'

She gasped. 'No! Let me think. I'll come to London. On Thursday.'

She walked quickly away from him. She sat in the driving seat, her heart pounding.

I won't go, she thought. The children were chattering, demanding praise and comment about the concert. But if she didn't go he'd turn up again in the village, at Senhouse even. How did he get here? She snapped at the children to shut up. How the hell, how the bloody hell had Mike Roper found his way here?

There was a letter from him. Someone must have told him how to address the envelope correctly: Mrs H. C. W. Sennen, Senhouse, near Halemouth. It was written half in sorrow, half in bewilderment, not at all that she could detect in anger. So it would be all the more difficult. A monumental row, she thought, a showdown, some dramatically unrestrained insults—that would finish the affair in the right spirit, since her disappearance had not managed to be final. But if he was going to be as sentimental, as drooling, as repulsively soppy as at their last meeting, it would be hard to make him realise that Jane Shore was dead, and forgotten by Venetia Sennen.

Venetia sat at breakfast with her hand to her cheek, and Hugh was concerned about her toothache, and went to telephone the dentist in Harley Street for her. That meant that she would have to keep the appointment. How lucky that no one could ask you to prove that something hurt.

Lindsay had been a bit strange the last few days. She was sitting across the table now frowning at Venetia. But she did not seem to mind the idea of fetching the children from school and giving them tea.

It was so silly, Venetia thought, for Mike to write about divorce and house hunting and her future relationship with his daughter. Under his randy and casual exterior he must have a soul like a blancmange. That glimpse of him in the village, in an environment where Jane would never appear, had reminded Venetia how impossible he was. Even his name—it was funny how Biffo, Jumbo or Dick could appear in *Jennifer's Diary* linked with titles and double barrels, while Mike, Pete and Dave were fit only for the cast of a student's rag week. There was a difference, one of degree so slight as to be unmeasurable, between those abbreviations and those used by the sort of person Venetia might leave Hugh for.

All those other times, the transformation in Venetia had begun almost before she reached Halemouth station—not so much in her appearance, but in her feelings. Jane's detachment from Venetia's preoccupation would flutter at the back of her mind, on the drive past the familiar village halls, community homes, shops selling local produce and other monuments to rural stability. She would act a part in the train if she met acquaintances who were going up for the day, and be bored by the preoccupations which when she was at home she shared. This time there was no such loosening of the daily chains. It was Venetia Sennen who descended from the train at Waterloo, and took a taxi to Harley Street for the unnecessary visit to the dentist. And as she opened obediently wide and rinsed the gritty disinfectant from her mouth, anger swelled like a balloon.

How dare he follow her to Senhouse? What right had he to intrude? The arrangement had been made as clear by him as by her; there had never been any question, she thought as she stared at the landscape projected on to the ceiling for the distraction of patients, that either Mike or Jane intended more than a one-dimensional relationship. So soon as he had dared to mention the fatuous plans he had concocted, she had brought the whole business to an end.

Venetia travelled by the underground from Great Portland Street to Ealing. It was the first time she had been in the office when it was being used as such, and the first time she consciously noticed all the legal paraphernalia, so different from that which she had occasionally seen from the client's chair in Lincoln's Inn, where the Sennen family papers were still kept in a tin box with the name painted on the outside, and where the law served, rather than threatened, the firm's clients. If Mike Roper managed with that narrow shelf of law books, she wondered whether Phipps, Phillips & Pipson really needed their many glass-fronted cabinets full of law reports and commentaries though of course books did furnish that room.

The office had a general air of poverty and seediness which had added to its attraction for Jane Shore. But it made even more ludicrous the idea that Venetia Sennen could have anything to do with it. The girl who seemed to be typist, receptionist and clerk was a scruffy seventeen-year-old, her beige, slightly pimpled chest revealed by a low-cut shirt; she smelt as though she could do with a wash.

'I'd like to see Mr Roper, please,' Venetia said coldly. The girl did not look up. Her long nail, with dirt showing through the chips in the red varnish, went down a list of names.

'Have you got an appointment?'

'He's expecting me. The name's Shore. Miss Shore.'

'He's got someone with him.'

'I'll wait.' Venetia sat down, uninvited, on a rickety wooden chair. The little room was immediately below the attic bedroom. There was equipment for making tea and several dirty cups; the typewriter's enamel was flaking and piles of papers and letters lay on every surface including the floor. On the wall was a calendar with a picture of a naked girl, advertising car tyres. The window looked out on to the same small yard with which Venetia had become familiar; from this floor, one storey nearer the ground, she could see that there was actually a wooden gate leading into it. There seemed to be not only the same amount but the identical pieces of waste paper littering it that she had seen in March.

A youth came into the little room, handed a pile of letters to the girl, stared at Venetia and left without saying a word. She took out a cigarette, and reached past the girl for the empty coffee tin that seemed to be the ashtray. The low drone of voices in the next room became louder. A woman could be heard shrilly complaining about Mike's slowness. The law's delays, Venetia thought, should hardly surprise anyone who entered this office.

The door opened, and the voluble woman came out still grumbling. She started down the stairs, muttering abuse as she went. Mike Roper called through the open door, 'You can be off now.'

'There's someone here for you,' the girl said, slamming drawers with obvious eagerness to be off.

'I can't see anyone now.'

'She says you're expecting her.'

'The cat's mother has come to see you,' Venetia drawled.

She gave the girl the look she usually reserved for convicted juvenile offenders when she was on the bench.

'Jane!' He came through from the front room, his face glistening with sweat, the knot of his tie pulled below the open top button of his shirt, his trousers wrinkled on his thighs, the nylon of his shirt showing the shape of the vest beneath it.

'It's about my will,' she said loudly. She went into his room, and shut the door behind her. She stood listening to the noises next door. Soon they heard the girl and the articled clerk going down the outside stairs together, giggling. Mike held out his arms to her. She ignored them, and sitting down on his client's chair, lit another cigarette from the stub of the first. She said, 'Well?'

'Well what?'

'You made me come here today.'

'Only so that we could talk in peace. Oh, it's been such a long time! You naughty girl—'

She thought, this is the first time I've really seen this man since the first evening. Whenever I was here I was watching myself in another role, having the alternative life, the sort of life Lindsay leads. How could I, he looks so—so common! She stared coldly at him.

'Jane, we must talk. About ourselves, our future.'

'Look here, Michael.' She drew in her breath. They had been on a desert island; when they were shut into that room, the concept of being common, the knowledge of what her friends would think of him, disappeared. But now she'd have to be on a desert island to let him touch her. 'We don't have a future, not together, not anything to do with each other,' she said. 'That's the only reason I came today, to get that into your head. It's all finished, such as it was, all over. Do you understand?'

'But we love each other.'

She laughed. 'Don't be ridiculous. You were the one who made it perfectly clear that all you wanted was a straight sex thing. You knew perfectly well that it was all we had.'

'That may be true, at the beginning. But I realise how unfair I was to you. I was a right bastard, expecting you—anyway, now I know better.'

'That's up to you. All I can say is that for me it meant nothing more than that—nothing at all. You haven't anything to do with my real life, you never could have. I was tight, I suppose, when I came here the first time, tight or overexcited—'

I was intoxicated by liberty, she thought. The strangeness of that evening at Palfrey & Blackwood's party, when nobody knew who I was, and I knew I'd never see any of them again. I remember the words running through my head, I kept thinking, 'He needn't ever know' and 'he' was both of them—Hugh, who need never know what I was up to, and this man, who'd never know who I was.

'I didn't mean anything at first, except sex,' he said

humbly. He was perched on the edge of his desk. His hand, when he lifted it, left a print on the scratched metal surface. 'I only came to love you later.'

'Love! You didn't even know me, you know nothing about me except what my body's like!' She spoke more frankly than she could ever have done before, but was conscious of the new inhibition she felt, now that he knew who, in real life, she was. 'And I don't know you either,' she added. At home she would have made a mental contact with a man before so much as accepting a drink from him; she would have put forward her feelers, her politenesses, and offered clues in return. She had never asked Mike Roper anything. As far as she was concerned, he didn't exist as a personality at all. 'I don't even know if you are married.'

'But I told you often about Samantha.'

'So you did, I'd forgotten.' He would have a daughter called Samantha. Venetia, who always felt that she had suffered from her 'fancy name' had chosen unexceptionably prosaic names for her own children. Harriet had already listed many she would have preferred, from Abigail to Zoe.

'And my wife doesn't count. We haven't anything in common.'

'Are you going to tell me she doesn't understand you?'

'Well, she doesn't. And she won't care, you needn't worry about her.'

'I don't worry about her because I don't expect ever to give her a moment's thought. It's all over between us, Mike. I don't love you, I never did, I don't want to see you again.' It's certainly true, she thought, that I don't love him. Actually, I think I hate him—I hate his turning from an escape route into an intrusion. She stared at his flushed face, and compared it with Hugh's, hard and bony where Mike's was soft and fat, and reddened not by emotion but by the weather. Hugh would never involve a woman in this tiresome scene. Mike had buried his face in his hands, and

139

now he made an effort, he rubbed his eyes and drew the back of his hand over his wet forehead, and pulled up the knot of his tie.

'Then there's another matter,' he said, 'if that's decided.'

Relieved, she said, 'Well, I'm glad that's over.'

'The question of money.'

'Oh, the enamel egg?'

'It isn't sold.'

'Thank God for that,' she cried, ready to forgive him.

'It's incomplete. There should be a figurine inside it.'

'What a relief.'

'What?'

'To have it back before it's missed!'

'I need the figurine. Have you got it?'

'Don't be silly. I need the egg—someone's going to look at the collection next week.'

'But I need the money.'

'Bad luck,' she said.

'I don't know.' He stood up, his face suffused again, and spoke vigorously, not pleading now. 'You're a right bitch, you are. Making out you fancy me, coming on the fiddle—fine that would sound, to your fellow justices, wouldn't it? Oh yes, don't worry, I know you are a magistrate, simply confirms my opinion of the lay bench, that does. You liked it fine when nobody knew it was you, didn't you? Well, I like it too, and I'm damned if I'll have everything buggered up because a layabout blackmails me and a tart won't keep her bargains. You're a tart. A whore.' The accent of his childhood was more pronounced in his voice as he abused her. She cowered away from him. 'You can bloody well pay before you get out to your safe little bourgeois hidey hole. At least I'll have that.'

She said in a little, cold voice, 'Where is the enamel egg?'

'Where you won't find it. I gave it to my Samantha with chocolates inside it at Easter. Put that in your bloody pipe and smoke it.'

'It isn't yours.'

'It doesn't sound as though it was yours either, come to that.'

Her inhibitions had not only been sexual. The freedom to lose one's temper was put aside with childish things, even shouting at the children made her guilty, and to let herself go with anyone else had always seemed out of the question. Mike was providing a brief final liberation. 'You bastard,' she shouted. 'You sod. You shit.' She couldn't think of any more powerful epithet. 'I hate you, Michael Roper, I despise your vulgar mind and your sweating face. I wouldn't let you touch me again if you were the last man on earth. I wouldn't let you lick my boots.'

'Secondhand language, secondhand mind,' he jeered.

'I think,' she said softly, staring at him, 'I think that I would like to kill you.'

'Melodrama.' He was right, she thought, or would have been, if she hadn't meant it. She would really like to kill him now, she could imagine doing it, having the purpose and ruthlessness. She did not think her hand would falter on the trigger or the knife. She would pour the poison in his cup and watch him die. She was astonished at herself. She trembled with hatred.

'I'm going,' she said. 'I'd better not ever see you again.' She went through the door, and left it open behind her. She slammed the outer door of the office, and ran down the stairs, smelling, for the first time, the dust and dirt. When she was outside the front door, she felt a weight of self-disgust lifting from her back. That's over, she thought, just one more hurdle.

Venetia was accustomed to having to extricate herself from inconvenient situations. In her catalogue of well-

141

known emotions, this one would have appeared beside the feeling of doom on days when she was due to go into hospital, of dismay when the washing machine broke down, and of disorientation when she was about to leave home for a long journey. From the days when, as a girl, she could avoid doing what she had promised by claiming that her mother wouldn't let her—and Harriet had already learned the same trick—to the occasions in adult life when she would trot out lame excuses for not after all organising children's parties for charity, stalls at jumble sales or open afternoons at Senhouse for the local historical society, her life had consisted of making advance, immediately regretted, commitments, and of wriggling out of them. Retrieving the Fabergé egg was not exactly a commitment; but the invention of excuses felt as familiar as though it were.

She found the Ropers' address in the telephone book with an ease which amused her when she thought what trouble it must have been to Mike to trace where she lived. She went there at once, but nobody answered her ring, and as she stood on the landing a woman toiled up to the flat above and told her that everyone was out until the child came out of school. She had some lunch in a café, and wandered round the refuge of W. H. Smith and Woolworth, identical to their branches in Halemouth, and tried on a dress in a boutique. At half past three she was waiting outside the Ropers' front door again.

The house was a converted Edwardian villa. The Ropers' flat was on the middle of three floors, with its front door set in a plywood partition which had been erected against the banisters. The landing floor was unpolished parquet and the wallpaper pattern showed through the thin layer of paint which an amateur had applied. There were four empty milk bottles, clean enough for immediate re-filling, and some canvassers' leaflets were lying on the window sill. The window was stained glass and looked out on to the back of another house. There was a smell of old frying and cabbage. Venetia could hear the television, with the familiar tunes of children's hour. She wished herself in her own home to listen to the safe sound of Jackanory. She rang the bell, and immediately heard the flushing of a lavatory on the other side of the plywood partition.

The door was opened by a dark-skinned woman. Beside her was a small child, with pale smooth skin and black eyes and hair.

'I am sorry,' Venetia said, backing towards the stairs. 'So sorry—I must have come to the wrong house. I was looking for Mrs Roper.'

'I am Mrs Roper,' the woman said. Her face and voice were calm, competent, reliable. She must be a nurse, Venetia thought, a ward sister.

She said, 'May I come in for a moment?'

Mrs Roper glanced at her, and then backwards into the room; then, her face expressionless, she stood aside. Venetia went straight into the Ropers' living-room; once, presumably, the master bedroom of the house, it was, she thought, surprisingly pleasant, clean and without the food smell of the landing, and within the obvious limits of money and time shortages, nicely furnished in an artless style. Venetia looked rapidly around the room, and noticed both the damp stains and the ornaments, and the not quite closed door leading into a bedroom. She stood with her back to the place where a fire would once have been.

Christine Roper waited. The child stood half behind her mother, sucking her thumb, her large eyes fixed on the visitor. 'I wondered—is your husband at home?' Venetia said.

'No, not till much later. Did you want to see him?'

'Yes, well, both of you really. It's easier,' Venetia stated, 'if one can see the husband and wife together.'

'What is this? Are you selling something?'

'In a way.'

'In that case—I don't think—'

'I must say,' Venetia said faintly, 'I don't feel most awfully well.' She sat down on the chair beside her, and dropped her head between her knees. She heard Christine Roper's footsteps coming nearer. 'You'd better fetch a glass of water, Samantha.' Soft breathing. Silence. The child coming back. Venetia looked up to see Christine Roper standing over her with a wet glass in her hand.

'Thank you.' She drank, spinning it out with small sips.

'Do you feel better now?' Calm, unconcerned, distant. Does she think I'm a confidence trickster? She'd be right at that.

'I think perhaps if I could lie down for a moment?' Get into the bedroom, see if it's there. How to mention it casually? 'Eaten something that disagreed with me, I'm afraid. I did it at Easter too. Too many eggs.' Inane laugh.

'You look quite well.' One could imagine her in a white coat, one of the caring professions; a physiotherapist, or a psychiatric social worker. A nice-looking woman, too nice for him. And he'd talked about her as though she didn't matter at all. 'Who are you?'

'My name is Shore. Mrs Shore.' That would scare him, if he got to hear of it later.

'Mummy!' The child's high voice, London accent, shy 'I know who she is!'

'Hush, dear, that's not polite.'

'No, Mummy,' insistent, demanding. 'Listen Mummy, do listen. It's Jane, Daddy's Jane, he told me about her. He said she was like that, he drew me a picture of her.'

'Go to your room, Samantha. Go at once. No, I don't want you to bring the picture, I have seen it if it's the one you put under your mattress; go now, and shut the door.' The child went into the other room, and her mother stood

144

immobile, watchful. 'I should have recognised you myself,' she said. 'He made a good likeness.'

Venetia quartered the room with her eyes; on top of bookcases several ornaments but no Fabergé egg; not in the glass-fronted sideboard; not on the window sill. Damn, damn, she thought, double damn. That portrait—too late now to say one was collecting for the lifeboats, which would have come naturally, from long practice; too late to be selling encyclopaedias.

'What have you to say to me?' Christine Roper said. Venetia looked at her briefly and dropped her eyes. A clever woman, a good woman; self-contained and proud. She must know that Mike had a mistress, had seen this sketch he'd made of her. Does she think I want to marry—?

'Nothing,' Venetia said. 'I made a mistake.'

'Nothing about Mike?'

'No. No. I'll go.' She got up, forgetting to seem unsteady on her feet. 'You needn't mention that I came. I won't come again.'

'You won't come here again,' Christine Roper said, with hardly a note of query in her voice.

'No, I won't be seeing him anywhere. I'm sorry. Truly. I'm very sorry.' Impossible to ask for the egg, impossible to force one's way into either bedroom. If the choice was between thinking up an explanation for Hugh, and one for this proud, withdrawn woman, she would manage the former more easily.

It was raining outside now, heavy drops soaked on impact through Venetia's black dress. She walked along the street, smelling the dust as the rain fell on it, scuffing with her feet the bark flakes from the plane trees. It was not that she minded that Christine Roper was being deceived by Mike, and that Venetia herself was 'the other woman'. In the abstract, she might almost like the idea, the adventure, of being 'the other woman'. But that she had never thought to wonder about her—that worried her. She had known perfectly well, of course, that Mike was married, and she had not given a damn, any more than she thought of Hugh as a cuckold. It had not entered her head. But Christine deserved better than that. Venetia was ashamed.

No taxis appeared to venture into this district, and Venetia went down into the underground station. The episode was over, and the only problem left was to finish it tidily, so that nothing could be held against her later.

The Fabergé egg, and, of course, almost forgotten, the Chinese water buffalo; what hope was there of Hugh not noticing that they were missing? He could walk the upstairs passages for a year without giving more than an automatic glance at the cabinets which lined their walls, in exactly the same way as he could admire her dress, and be unable, a moment later, to remember its colour. But if he actually looked, if he thought about it, he knew down to the last miniature ivory elephant, of the twenty-five which fitted into a thimble-sized box, what should be there.

If more were to disappear, it might be plausible that those two objects were gone. After all, the plumber, the slater and the electrician had all visited the house more than once in the last months. Or could one blame the children? Would their denials be convincing?

If only, Venetia thought, I could simply go into a couple of shops in the Burlington Arcade and replace the damned things. Hugh would be unlikely to do more than raise an eyebrow at his own imprecise memory. Money, she thought; the whole trouble is there in the first place because I didn't have any money.

Palfrey & Blackwood had paid two hundred pounds down for the book, with vague remarks about royalty percentages. It had seemed like riches at the time. Hugh's system was not ungenerous, for he believed he must do what he had promised in the Church of England's modernised marriage service, and share all his worldly goods with his wife. Unfortunately this meant not giving her an allowance, but having a joint bank account with her. Unfortunately too he was a great one for making his figures tally, and since he had no objection to explaining his own expenditure to his wife, indeed insisted at boring length in showing her how he had spent all the money he had drawn out, he expected similar details from Venetia. In the first years of their marriage it had been awkward to buy him presents because Venetia felt she was simply giving his own money back to him. Since she had taken up embroidery it had been easier, as she regarded her embellishment of the Senhouse furniture as being by way of a gift to Hugh. This year he would receive the third in a series of covers for the dining-room chairs, all different designs in the same muted shades to replace the worn brown leather.

The trips to London had mostly been explainable by the dentist. A few illicit daytime visits to Mike's had been 'lost', expensive though both the petrol and the train fare had become, in the housekeeping money. But the illusion of wealth provided by two hundred pounds of her very own had led to the indulgence of extravagant tastes which would be hard to square with Hugh who lived, on the whole, a self-denying life. He accepted the need for new clothes, but not for very many and not for very good ones. On the other hand, he did not recognise their age or quality; he never knew whether he had seen them before or not. And what with those new clothes and other tiny sums dissipated on taxis, meals and the pleasure of having spare money, the two hundred pounds had been spent sooner than Venetia would have thought possible. And why, she thought, not by any means for the first time, as we give the world the impression of wealth that living at Senhouse must produce when I never have any spending money at all? The only hope was those mysterious royalties.

At Green Park underground station she paused. There was no need to go to the Country Club. She had joined it when she saw an advertisement in one of the magazines she read in the hairdressers, just at the time when she realised that she would need an address. Without an address she would not exist; Jane Shore would never be able to acquire a bank account or a credit card or even her putative royalties. The Country Club had advertised that it provided an elegant London address, and bedrooms when required, with guaranteed discretion, and it offered an introductory membership for a reduced sum of money. It sounded just the job. She hadn't liked the place. It smelt as though fresh air had always been the aerosol variety, and the artificial elegance both of the interior decoration and of the few other members she had caught sight of was not the sort of thing which made Venetia feel at ease. Her subscription would have run out by now, and presumably that relentlessly ladylike receptionist would have forwarded any letters to the Royal Counties Bank. She would go there. Or would it be better to ring up Palfrey & Blackwood? She stood outside the Ritz Hotel and dithered. If she had been armoured in Jane Shore's personality she would have gone into the hotel and had a drink at the bar, brandy or whisky, the sort of drink which men like Hugh did not like their women to order in public. Venetia did not quite like to go in. She felt equally inferior to the guests dressed by Dior and by the local market stall; her own dull tidiness fell uneasily between either of the two necessary extremes. She walked along to a café where she could have a sandwich and a cup of coffee. At least, she thought, in the lounge of the Crown and Anchor in Halemouth they know who I am and what I'm for.

Fortified by food she went into a telephone box in Piccadilly tube station. Some people with shaven heads and temple bells were marching around the crowded pavements, chanting, weaving skilfully between the shrill children of a French school party. Some English girls in old-fashioned uniform gave the disorganised French a scornful glance as they bypassed the scrum. Going home from school time already? Venetia checked the time. She would have to get a move on.

She rang the publishers and asked to speak to Guinevere.

'Miss Shore? I'm so glad you rang, we'd been trying to get in touch with you. Are you in town?'

'Yes, I really only wanted to know—'

'Could you come into the office? A bit late today, tomorrow perhaps?'

'No, I just wanted to ask about royalties. I've been away. Have there been any?'

'I think John sent you a cheque the other day. I'm afraid I can't recall the exact sum. But Miss Shore, we wanted to ask you—one of the characters in *A Pleasure to Come*—it's terribly awkward but it seems that the name you used for the narrator, the descendant of Lady Babs you know—it never occurred to us that there could be anybody—but we've had a letter from some solicitors—John doesn't think anything will come of it, but if you could just look in at the office and—'

'I'm so sorry, I can't—' Would the money never run out? Just as Venetia wondered this she heard the pips, and through them Guinevere anxiously asking whether she had enough change, and what was the number of the box she was calling from, she would dial— Finished. Cut off. Venetia put the receiver down and moved aside for an angry-looking negro who had been closely watching her every move through the glass.

That's all she needed; a libel action. That was just dandy.

She tried to remember the wording of the relevant clause in the contract she had signed with the name of Jane Shore, nearly two years ago. Had she indemnified Palfrey & Blackwood or something, against the expense of damages? She reminded herself that they didn't know who she was either.

The Royal Counties Bank's door would be closed by now. She joined the back of the queue for telephone boxes again. At least, thank goodness, they answered the telephone. The girl took a lot of convincing that she really was Jane Shore, and maintained to the end that she would get the sack for giving information about clients' accounts on the telephone. But Venetia made up a convincing enough story, and as the girl said, the sum involved was very small. There had been a payment in from Palfrey & Blackwood in April of two pounds sixty-three pence. But please please would Miss Shore never let on that she had told her.

So that was that. No money, no replacement egg or water buffalo. Venetia took another tube train to Waterloo.

Venetia had been expected home for dinner, but changed her mind while she was on the way to Waterloo, and took herself to see a pornographic film about lesbians in Hong Kong. Then she ate shrimps and drank stout at a high marble bar in one of those establishments where the lone woman is treated with a mixture of indulgence and suspicion. Her train got her to Halemouth after ten, and she drove slowly home. She missed the feeling of returning renewed from her adventures and the better able to enjoy her daily life. Infidelity, she thought, used to do her a world of good.

She put her car away in the garage, and paused to sniff the country air before going quietly into the house. With any luck Hugh and Lindsay would be asleep. The lights were off in the drawing-room and the hall, and she tiptoed into the pantry to pour herself some whisky, which she drank standing there in her stockinged feet; she could feel their swollen flesh shrinking against the cool tiles.

It was with dismay that Venetia heard sounds from upstairs. They were still up, damn, oh damn. But they hadn't heard her come in. Hugh was talking to Lindsay, and clattering crockery, it seemed. Crockery? she thought. She went softly to the bottom of the stairs. The light was on in the far passage, the other end of the house from the bedrooms they now used. The passage had been turned into a sort of gallery by Hugh's grandfather, with glass-fronted mahogany cases lining the walls, and plinths above each door on which stood marble busts and ivory statues. The doors were those of bedrooms now rarely occupied, except in games of hide and seek and the battles of model soldiers for which undisputed floor space was required. One of the rooms was called the sewing-room, and held the ironing-board and the machine once used by the woman who came to do the Senhouse mending. Another had apples stored in racks; in a third room rose petals and lavender were left to dry on newspapers.

The glass cabinets housed the collection made by the ancestor who had bought Senhouse. He had been a captain of merchant ships; from the far-flung lands whence his employers had profited, he gathered his hoard throughout a long career: porcelain and jade from the coasts of China, silks and spice jars, shells and corals; curiosities from dealers, stolen goods from middlemen, embroideries from craftswomen, antiquities from tomb robbers. In the Baltic ports he purchased the treasures of refugees. In the Mediterranean he collected relics of the classical past. Cases and trunk loads were accumulated in attics and stables and warehouses, until he retired at last to spend his remaining years gloating. Family legend described him arranging and rearranging his goodies, polishing, stroking and hand-ling them like a miser. He had used the main rooms of the house as his store. Entering his living-room must have been like walking into a treasure house.

Hugh's grandfather had been a traveller too, on a less magnificent scale. He had set out to see objects whose description he knew, unlike the avid collector of random treasures. He planned his itineraries to include specific museums, organised every day of his journeys to use the time to full advantage—a gallery in the morning, a church in the afternoon, an evening in the hotel to write up his notes. In Hugh's library there were several volumes of his travel diaries, as dull and uninspired as their writer must have been. It was this grandfather who had brought the Fabergé egg. His additions had been planned, to fill gaps in the sequence. But the beauty came from the things which the uneducated sailor had seen and loved and wanted and acquired. One could sense, indefinably, the difference between an object needed by a pedant and its neighbour desired by an amateur.

It had been the pedant who moved the collection from its scattered shelves and niches in the downstairs room, and had constructed the museum-like cabinets which now housed everything. It perhaps pleased him that nobody looked at things with spontaneous admiration any more, or picked up a jade to stroke its smoothness, or saw with unplanned relish the unexpected sunlight on the bloom of a black mother of pearl shell from the South Seas. He preferred attention to be instructed. In the same way he had reorganised the gardens, scattering lead plaques with Latin botanical names in the flower beds, taming the shrubberies, and regularising the vistas. Symmetry, he had told his children, was all. The gardens must have been magnificent. Hugh regretted now that the shrubs were growing together into impenetrable, fairy-tale thickets, and that neglect was hastening their death. It saddened him that they could not keep the place up properly. Venetia thought Senhouse looked beautiful in an undisciplined, romantic way. In any case, Hugh's life as a working farmer left him no time to stop the decay, and his income did not enable him to pay anyone else to do it. But he worried, as about so many things, about the state of his gardens.

How typical, Venetia thought as she leant weakly against the banisters, that she should come home after such a day to find that Hugh was now, of all times, cleaning the shelves and washing the objects in the gallery. She could hear the soft splashing of soapy water; Lindsay must be there helping. She listened anxiously, but could hear nothing to suggest that Hugh had yet noticed any gaps in the collection. She had chosen carefully, when she had thought, in her self-confident mood of the earlier part of the year, that the odd piece here or there amongst so many could disappear unnoticed. She had told herself that they were in any case, virtually hers to sell. After all, Hugh said he shared his worldly goods with her. Unfortunately, it no longer felt like a good defence, her previous arguments dried upon her tongue. In Hugh's eyes, she would have stolen, not from him so much, as from the entity that was Senhouse. And how could she ever explain to him why she had needed the money?

Venetia crept on stockinged feet back to the kitchen and into the pantry. The dog flapped his feathery tail against the floor but was too lazy to move. Venetia pulled over a chair, and climbed on it to open the top part of the housemaid's cupboard. She took down the broken toaster, the one which Henry had kept using to see the trip switch on the main power box snapping up. Lucky, she thought, that it always took her so long to take things for mending.

Where could she put it, out of sight? Eventually she went cautiously along the passage to the dining-room and plugged the toaster into a wall socket behind the sideboard. She fed the flex through the crack in the door of the little cupboard where tableclothes were kept, and pushed the linen back out of the way. She put the toaster in the cupboard. The door would nearly close.

Venetia tiptoed back to the door with her chair, and reached high to wrench the telephone wires from the junction box. Then she quietly put her chair back at the kitchen table and went outside.

Moving noisily, she walked across the yard and in at the kitchen door. The dog barked this time, but quickly stopped. She clattered her heels on the tiles, ran the tap and slammed the lids of the Aga. Then she clicked up the passage to the front of the house. She called 'Hullo' up the stairs.

'That you, darling? We're preparing for Dorothy Westbourne's visitation.'

'I'll be up in a minute.' She went into the drawing-room and noiselessly pressed the light switches down. Then she crept into the dining-room and pressed the toaster's switch. With a loud phut-click noise, the house was thrown into darkness. Hastily Venetia pushed the door as far shut as possible and went into the hall, where she was waiting when Hugh came down the stairs. There was a routine for electrical failures, which happened quite frequently at Senhouse; its equipment tended to cause mirth in visiting electricians.

'Sorry, darling,' Venetia said. 'All I did was switch on the drawing-room lights.'

'Not your fault.' Hugh held a match in front of him and made his way into the dining-room to light the candles which stood in the silver sticks. He handed one to Venetia. 'Tooth better?'

'Yes, thanks.'

'Come and hold the candle, will you?'

Venetia followed Hugh as he methodically flicked the drawing-room switches up. 'That should do it.' He went down the passage to fetch a chair, and Venetia stood near him as he climbed on it. The candle flame guttered in the draught from under the back door. 'Damn thing won't stay up,' he muttered. 'Can't understand it.' He got down. 'I'll have to turn off everything.' Venetia went round the house after Hugh. He switched off all the lights which had been on, the refrigerator, deep freeze and the boiler's time clock. Even then the trip switch would not stay open.

Hugh was not a man to give up easily, and it took him half an hour's fuming to surrender, and get himself to bed by candlelight. Lindsay had already disappeared into her room, relieved, probably, to be let off the rest of the boring task to which Hugh had set her. Venetia had not liked to leave Hugh to it, and stood around trying to seem helpful, shining the beam of her torch, which she had fetched from the car, into useful places.

Hugh usually fell asleep at once. Tonight he was too keyed up with frustration. He was not used to letting practical obstructions defeat him. Venetia felt that he was blaming her for the light failure, and was as annoyed as if he had not been justified. After all, he wasn't to know that he was right—his vexation was directed to some unspecified laxness not to a single, premeditated act.

'What did you do all day? You were back late,' he said.

'Oh, I thought I'd do a bit of shopping while I was there. And I went to see Carlina. She's pregnant again.' That was safe enough. Carlina had written that she was pregnant, and Hugh couldn't bear her and would never check. 'Everything all right here?'

'Mm, I was out most of the day. Had to go for some more barbed wire and I got waylaid at the club by Godfrey Pugh. He saw Lindsay in the Crown and Anchor with a man on Tuesday. Said she looked—well, I won't say what he said.'

'I can guess.'

'Don't you think it's about time she moved on, actually?'

'Where to? You know that Liz Wainwright has gone out to Colin? Didn't you see her photo in the paper on Sunday?'

'Well, Lindsay will have to stop sulking in the tent sometime.'

'Give her a bit longer. Perhaps if she met someone in Halemouth the other day....'

'Didn't sound very suitable, from what Godfrey said. Not that her men ever are very suitable. Godfrey thought he was a commercial traveller. He was called Roper, according to the barman.'

Venetia heaved herself around in the bed and pressed her head into the pillow.

'Of course,' Hugh went on, 'what Lindsay needs is a good roll in the hay. That would solve her problems. I'm almost tempted myself.' Venetia rolled away from him. He followed her across the wide bed. 'That's given me an idea,' he said.

'I've got the curse, sorry,' she said. 'Anyway, I'm exhausted.' She breathed regularly, willing him to sleep. Once he was snoring, she would be safe to get up without waking him. She lay in the ebony darkness. Without the usual light left on in the passage she could literally not see her hand before her eyes. I hate the dark, she thought. I must get a battery nightlight for the next power failure. No wonder people believed in ghosts, when they could never see beyond a candle's flame.

When Hugh was asleep, she would creep down to the back kitchen and bring the dog into the house. She could pretend in the morning that, what with the light failure and being so tired, she had left the door a little open. One sweep of his heavy tail across the table where the objects were lying, between soapy water and polish, would do for a good many of them. Would it be plausible for the dog to turn the table over on top of the debris, crushing some fragments so that no restorer could mend them? It wasn't good, but the best she could do.

If only Hugh would fall fast asleep. His breathing was still quiet. He would stir if she did. She lay listening to the silence. They were not in a flight path here, and rarely heard aeroplanes overhead. Guests from London sometimes complained that it was too peaceful for them to be able to rest. The owl hooted, and the siren of the train was just audible, wind-borne from the viaduct three miles away.

A thud along the corridor: a heavy book falling off the end of Henry's bed. He moaned and spoke in his sleep, but she could not distinguish the words. Henry still insisted that his bedroom door should be left open all night. He would scream if he woke up to this darkness. There was a rapid scuttling of little feet in the rafters: a mouse, or a squirrel. When she had first moved to Senhouse Venetia had stayed awake at nights for fear of the animal life which populated the interstices of her new home, but she knew now that the cat kept them from venturing below the roof space or above the foundations; the only mice she saw were the ones their predators brought in dead.

Wheeze; gurgle; pause. Hugh was snoring at last. Venetia cautiously swung her feet over the edge of the bed, feeling for her slippers. Her eyes were shut, for opening them did not lessen the darkness.

What was that? She froze, listening, straining her eyes, wide now. One of the children fumbling towards the bathroom? No, the sound had come from the other direction, at the far end of the house from Lindsay's bedroom and the children. There was someone in the gallery! She sat like a stone, listening. For several moments there was no sound. She must have been imagining it, she chided herself—her conscience at work. Then suddenly there was another faint noise. Was it something dropping on to the floor? There was someone there, she was sure of it. And she was equally sure that Lindsay had not come past her bedroom door.

She felt like collapsing, giggling with relief. The burglar could not have come on a better night, he was just what she needed, an answer to prayer. Good luck to him. After all, if she'd been asleep, the minimal sounds he had made would never have woken her, he could have cleaned the house right out and kidnapped the children while he was about it.

The children! She had been so intent on her own preoccupation that she had forgotten her chief responsibility.

What if he wanted—after all, one heard such terrifying stories nowadays—was he after Henry and Harriet? She leant over towards Hugh, and gently put one hand over his mouth, shaking his shoulder with the other.

In his sleep, he fought to move her hands. How strong he was, even dreaming. She put her mouth to his ear, and whispered desperately, 'Hugh, Hugh, wake up.'

He woke very suddenly, one moment thrashing dopily against the interfering body, the next upright, alert. 'What is it?'

'Sssh.' She clapped her hand over his mouth, and he whispered again, 'What's the matter?'

'There's someone in the gallery. Listen.' They sat rigid, side by side, straining to hear. For a long moment there was no sound. 'You were dreaming,' he began to say. At that moment he heard the door of one of the glass-fronted cabinets creak as it opened, and he swung his legs over the side of the bed. He clicked the switch of his bedside light, forgetting that there was no power. He whispered urgently, 'Where's the torch?'

'I left it in the bathroom. Here's the matches. But be quiet.'

She was terrified now. Her worst night fears were coming true. Hugh lit the candle, and tiptoed to the chair. He pulled his trousers over his pyjamas and thrust his bare feet into shoes.

'What are you going to do?' she whispered.

'What do you think?' He walked silently across to the door of his dressing-room. Venetia sat in the traditional position of wives, waiting, hands over mouth, eyes wide and frightened, to be protected. She heard the minuscule sound of Hugh unlocking the door of one of his wardrobes. He kept his guns upstairs because on the ground floor it was too damp. Sometimes when he woke to see rabbits on the lawns, he shot at them through his open window.

The lock had been put on the door, years after Venetia started nagging him to secure the weapons against the children, when he last renewed his firearms certificate. The new chief constable was very nervous about young burglars getting hold of guns.

She heard a click, as he cocked the shotgun. Then silence: he must be creeping out of the other door of the dressing-room. He's always said that he would shoot an intruder in his house and been certain that no jury would convict him of a crime. Venetia doubted whether a representative jury would feel equally strongly that Hugh's home was his castle. But now she was glad he did.

Venetia cautiously got out of the bed. She felt for her dressing-gown, and her slippers. Funny, that these rarely used garments should seem necessary. It made those old films seem more plausible, she thought irrelevantly, where the heroine always had to tie a wrapper tightly round herself before the action could proceed. Venetia had often sat in front of the screen thinking that in real life she would never wait to cover that glamorous nightgown, those chic pyjamas. But now she did up every last button on her own armour.

She drew the curtains open, and it became possible to make out the shapes of the furniture. Feeling her way, she went to the door of the room, open already as it was left every night. She thought she would bar the way along the passage to the children's bedrooms.

There was no sound. Hugh must be stalking his prey. What would he say? 'Hands up', perhaps? Would he really shoot? Did he want to wound, or only to drive away? How little she knew him.

Venetia moved a little way along the passage, and stood at the top of the stairs. A faint illumination came through the long window, and she could see the outline of the banisters, and the clock on the half-landing.

Suddenly she heard a shout—Hugh's voice—and the sound of running feet thudding along in the distance. He was making for the back stairs. She could hear him skidding down them, and then his heels on the back passage. She went softly down the front stairs. There was Hugh following. He'd broken the gun, and was carrying it as he would when shooting a permissible quarry.

'Stop,' she called, 'let him go, you've driven him off. Hugh, stop.'

'I'm going after him.'

'No—let him get away. It's not safe, he might—'

'Don't be silly.'

'But Hugh—'

'I'm not going to let some bastard get away with breaking into my house,' he whispered furiously, his voice receding as he went out into the yard, following the intruder who had escaped through the back door, which had been open, presumably as he had himself left it. The dog was barking now, leaping at the door of the back kitchen, his nails scrabbling against the woodwork. Venetia took a candle and went to get him, and clipped on the lead, and then holding tightly on to the plaited leather, preceded by a panting, eager retriever, she followed Hugh and his quarry out into the night.

The moon had appeared, round, streaked with clouds. She could see where to go in the cold light. There was no sound or sign of the two men. She crossed the yard, and went round the side of the house. The honeysuckle and the cut grass gave out a heavy scent. She heard the susurrant ears of corn, and the squeal of a nocturnal bird. Her little cat dashed across the path. There was nothing to be seen on this, the western side of the house, and she moved round to the long south front.

Hugh was there, walking with a steady sportsman's stride across the grass, and the dog strained to follow him, but Venetia stood still, clutching the lead and waiting. So would Hugh walk across stubbled fields in the autumn, his gun broken under his arm, the dog at his heel; so would she wait, the shepherd's pie in the hay box in the back of the car, the game bag at her feet. How bizarre to be here in flimsy nylon instead of tweed, to be sheltered by the walls of her own house instead of some shack or hide, to see, instead of the pale blue and tawny landscape of the harvested fields, this uncanny, dreamy vista of grey and silver, the yellow moon which drained all other tints displaying the only colour. She could distinguish the darker shape of the long flower beds and the silhouette of the trees which surrounded the garden. Framed in their symmetrical mass rose the stacked rhomboids of the pagoda.

And there, running towards it, inexorably pursued by its owner, ran the stranger; and momentarily, to Venetia, did not look strange at all.

Hugh was gaining on him. The man wasted his lead by getting caught in the barrier of the shrubbery, parts of which had become impenetrable. Hugh knew that he could eventually move only towards the lake, or back to the house, and walked inflexibly on. The man was by the bridge which led to the pagoda.

He was at bay. She could not see the details of his dark figure, but it looked as though he turned, and raised his arm, and brought it sharply down. Hugh ducked, and put his right arm quickly up to protect his head. The man had thrown something at him. He was going to throw again. Hugh cocked his gun and brought it up to his shoulder. The man was throwing, he was turning to run again, at the same moment as Hugh's gun banged, shockingly loudly. He must have missed, for the man was still moving. Now she could not see him. Hugh had turned and was walking back towards the house. Venetia let the dog off the lead, and he ran to fawn at Hugh's feet.

'That's settled him,' Hugh said. He broke the shotgun, and let the cartridges fall into his palm.

'You didn't hit him?' Venetia said.

'Don't think so. Only with the odd pellet if I did. He was too far away. But I doubt if he'll come back.' He sounded pleased with himself.

'Cave man,' she said.

'What do you expect?' he answered. Venetia shivered, and crossed her arms across her chest.

'To think I used to dance in strapless dresses on nights like this, out of doors. Do you remember?' she said.

Hugh's past only concerned him as an aspect of his family's history. 'Come on, it's cold. Maddening that we'll have to wait till daylight to see what's been touched.' They went in and he took care to bolt and lock the outside doors.

'Didn't you do this last night?' he said. 'The man must have got in through one of these doors.'

'I suppose, what with the dark and all, I might have forgotten,' she said. She could remember standing on the chair by the telephone wires, noticing that she had not pushed the bolts and chain across, and reminding herself to do it later. But she had not done it later.

Venetia offered to make tea, but Hugh said he was tired and would go straight back to bed. She made herself cocoa, and huddled against the Aga to thaw herself out. Hugh took this sort of thing awfully calmly, she thought. He objected to the unauthorised entry to his house because it violated his sense of property. Her own feelings were much less practical, less definable, though certainly as atavistic as his; her house was a sort of sanctuary which must be private, entered only by invitation and then only in limited areas. She did not really think of Senhouse as hers in an objective, title deed and property tax sense, and when she took some of its ornaments to sell she was emotionally, if not intellectually, aware that she was stealing. But the idea of a stranger in her lair upset her all the same. She would not feel as readily as Hugh that the episode was over. She would not sleep so quickly and easily.

Hugh was milking by six the next morning. When Venetia got up she found him in the long gallery replacing the pieces from the collection on the shelves. He held up a malachite bowl.

'I found this on the lawn. You'll have to come and help me hunt in the bushes. There seem to be one or two things missing.'

'Have you rung the police?'

'Tommy Clark is away, I think. Just as well to speak to a chap one knows.' His face was even redder than usual. He added, 'I'm not too sure. What do you think? After all, there was no harm done.'

'But Hugh, I should have thought you would—even last night—'

'Yes, well, it would have meant going past the fellow to get downstairs to the telephone. But now ... after all, I did take a shot at the man ...'

'I see. Least said soonest mended, you think?'

Hugh did not answer, and Venetia went down to lay the breakfast in a stupor of sleepiness and depression, unplugging her chaos-creating toaster on the way. The children bickered about whose turn it was for a particular plate and cup which were infinitesimally different from the others. Harriet screamed at the noise of the coffee grinder. Henry squeezed processed cheese from the wrong end of the tube and Venetia snapped at him. Lindsay came in from the yard and waited for coffee with her bottom on the corner of the table. A crust had fallen on the floor and she pushed it aside with her foot. Who does she think will have to pick it up, Venetia wondered.

Hugh took the children to school. Lindsay sat sipping, with her hair trailing on the smeared table. Venetia made meaningful, sharp noises as she stacked the crockery into the machine. But Lindsay did not even move when Venetia took her cup and wiped the table in front of her. 'What's the matter?' Venetia asked impatiently.

'Come out in the garden, I want to talk to you.'

'Why not here?'

'Hugh might come back. He's going to give me a lift into Halemouth. I want to go to a travel agent's.'

Venetia poured herself the remains of the coffee and went out into the garden. It looked like an uncorrupted Eden. The tiny magnolia, planted for Venetia's old age, had one flower on it.

'This grows so slowly, it will be years before it looks like anything. Come and see the children's trees.'

They went together along a flagged walk with long tufts of grass growing between the stones. At the end of the path, flanking an eighteenth-century sundial on which was carved the message 'tempus fugit' were a cherry and a syringa tree, labelled respectively on metal plaques with the two children's full names. 'They grow quicker than the children,' Venetia remarked, standing beneath the branches which met over her head. From this point in the garden they looked back towards the house which lay washed in sunlight amongst its shrubs and flowers. The herbaceous borders had been grassed over and edged with box hedges and lavender, so that the aspect must have been like that of earlier centuries, and it became possible to imagine a future for which it was worth planting trees. 'Hugh thought he might plant an avenue of yews leading to the lake,' Venetia said. 'It wouldn't look much for decades, but he's thinking of his posterity.'

'But they may not be here, you might not even stay here yourself.'

'Oh, I can't imagine us leaving here,' Venetia said. 'We'll both be carried out in our boxes, Hugh and I. I'm here for the rest of my natural life.'

Lindsay said, 'How smug you sound. Can you be so sure?'

Venetia laughed. 'Do you see Hugh leaving Senhouse?'

'No, but you might.'

'Thanks. But I shouldn't worry about that.'

'I know a man called Mike who might make you a bit less certain,' Lindsay said. Venetia put her hand out to the sundial, and her knuckles whitened as she gripped the metal pointer.

'What do you mean?' she whispered. 'What are you talking about?'

'He seemed pretty determined to find you. I don't know why, but you obviously do.'

'Did you tell him where to come?'

'No.'

'If that's true how do you know anything about him? What the hell have you been up to?'

Lindsay said sharply, 'I might ask you that.'

Venetia stared at her sister, her face suddenly drawn and the little veins on her cheek clearly marked against the pale skin. Then she sighed and said, 'What do you think?'

'I never thought it of you. Where did you meet him?'

'I shan't tell you and it was all a mistake, a very brief mistake and it's all finished.'

'What happened?'

'Three guesses. Man meets woman, and so on.'

'Did you really sleep with him?'

'I can't think why you sound so surprised. It's not as though you don't—'

'No, but that's different. I mean, you and Hugh—I thought you had something special going for you—you always gave the impression—'

'Yes, well, so we do,' Venetia said. 'That's why I don't want Mike Roper turning up here. Or anywhere.'

'Is it all over then?' Lindsay asked. Venetia nodded. 'I must say, I'm amazed. He picked me up in Halemouth. He thought I looked like you. Come to think of it, it might have been my fault at that, you know, I recognised the pagoda on the—'

'You haven't seen that?' Venetia interrupted. Her face was burning and her eyes felt as though they were bulging in their sockets.

'I haven't read it,' Lindsay lied. 'But he was asking in the information place, whether they knew where it was.' Venetia sat chewing her lips. 'Why's he so keen to find you? And why don't you want him to? I mean, if you told him—'

'Hugh isn't one of your trendy friends. What do you think would—? Anyway, I told you, it's all finished.'

'Not on his side.' They sat in silence for a moment. 'It seems so funny,' Lindsay went on. 'I mean, that sort of man. He's not exactly a—well, you know what I mean. He's not your usual type.'

'I don't know what you mean by "my usual type". There hasn't been anyone except Hugh for ten years. Mike Roper was a temporary aberration, it won't happen again. It's all over. Don't think I like having you sitting in judgment on me. I wouldn't say a word if I wasn't afraid that you'd do something like bringing him here and he'd start talking about divorce and his damned daughter.'

'Do you want to marry him?' Lindsay sounded astonished.

'*I* don't.'

'You mean he does? Is that why you finished with him?'

'If you must know, yes. I was having a—well, what you'd probably call a straight sex thing. Nothing to do with Hugh or the children or my own life at all. A roll in the hay, a bit of fun, whatever you like. But when he started getting emotional I dropped it. That's all.'

'You're rather brutal,' Lindsay objected. 'I mean, if he loved you— Don't imagine I'm like that, please. It sounds as though you've treated him rather badly. If you're going to embark on having affairs you mustn't just use people, even if they are called Mike and do look like bank clerks. The trouble is that you're such a snob, you probably don't think he feels things the way the upper classes do. You can't see past his accent and his background. I think he has a right to—'

'To what? Marriage? Honestly, this from you!'

'I may be liberated but I'm not cruel. You ought to talk it out, at least. That's why I'm going out to Africa. I've decided. Colin and I must have a chance to see each other, have a proper talk. If he really wants Liz now, at least I'll know where I stand.'

'Wouldn't it all be better left unsaid?' Venetia said, voicing a deeply felt belief. Hugh came round on to the terrace, and called Lindsay to get a move on, it was time to go. She walked towards the house.

'Will you be all right, darling?' Hugh called.

'Why ever not?'

'Oh, I just thought you might be feeling nervous. But I won't stay in Halemouth for lunch. We'll be back in a couple of hours.'

Venetia sat on a stone bench, and listened to the diminishing noise of the Land Rover as it went up the drive. The housework of the last few days was waiting, not to mention the neglected garden, the dirty car and the unanswered letters. In a moment she would push herself to begin.

The whisper from the shrubbery startled her into rigidity. She sat with her hands clasped across her thudding heart, feeling the skin on her cheekbones drawn tight, and her backbone cold.

'I must talk to you,' the voice repeated.

Very slowly she turned, and peered between the azaleas and rhododendrons. Mike Roper slowly pushed his way through the thick foliage. His clothes were streaked with mud and wetness, and his insensitive face, still pink but now unshaven and dirty, peered anxiously in her direction. 'Has he gone?'

'Who?'

'That maniac. Your husband—what did he think he was doing, shooting at me like that? Doesn't he know it's against the law? He could go to prison for years.'

'What about you, breaking into our house?' Venetia demanded, her alarm quickly replaced by anger.

'He fired in cold blood. Anyway, I need that figurine. Or something else at any rate. I told you, I've got to have the money. And I don't see why you should get away with it. Look what you've done to my life. I'm not going to let you escape scot free, Jane, Venetia, Mrs damn-your-eyes Sennen. You'll regret insulting me and frightening my daughter in her own home.'

'I must go in. What do you—'

'Not yet. I've got plenty else to say to you.'

Venetia stood up. 'I'm only going to get a cardigan. It's cold still. Shall I fetch you a cup of coffee? Hugh's gone out for a while with my sister.'

'In that case I'll come in too.'

'No! No, my cleaning woman is in the kitchen. She might look out and see you. Look, go and wait down there, beside the pagoda. I won't be long. Please, Mike.' She forced the fury out of her face.

'All right. But be quick. I'm bloody cold too. You might

170

bring me one of Lord Muck's sweaters while you're about it.'

As she turned the corner of the house she glanced back, and saw him going towards the rickety bridge.

Shut the dog up; upstairs quickly, quelling the urge to retire to the bathroom and lock herself in its sanctuary. The dressing-room: where had Hugh left the key? Was it still in his pocket? She felt through the trousers he had worn, and the pyjama top. Not there; not on his dressing-table, or the mantelpiece. That was that then. As a last try, she felt the cupboard door and found that it was not locked. The shotgun he had used last night; ammunition in his sock drawer. Make sure it was the right kind. Put the cartridges in her dress pocket. Down the front stairs, and out through the french window in the drawing-room. From here she could only see the top storeys of the pagoda, and he would not be able to see her. Lucky it was not really Mrs Best's day. The dog was barking in the back kitchen, she could hear it right through the house. The bantams had come round from the farmyard, and ran noisily away as she approached. Mike would not know enough about the country to be startled.

Safely across the lawn and into the shrubbery. If she followed the old path to the tennis court, edging round the lake, he would not be able to see her. The gun was heavy, and she had to hold it higher than was comfortable to prevent the barrel catching on trailing brambles. Lucky she had on rubber-soled shoes.

Her arm was aching by the time she had gone far enough. Just about here, she must be level with the bridge. With extreme caution she tiptoed between the bushes.

There he was, leaning over the balustrade. Didn't he feel how shaky it was?

Venetia pushed two cartridges into the gun barrels, and snapped it closed. He showed no sign of having heard the sound. Careful now: she placed her feet apart. Remember all those lessons, when Hugh still thought she might join in the shooting, instead of just praising his expertise. He was proud that she'd learnt so well, the first year of their marriage, boasted to his father about her eye, produced the target with the hole in the bullseye to prove it. She'd rather liked target shooting. But pregnancy had put her off shooting at living things; she could never explain the revulsion to Hugh, for he knew that there was no excuse for a carnivore to flinch at providing her own meal, but she had become the sort of wife whose only share was to hang the contents of the bag to putrefy in the larder.

One did not forget how to shoot, she told herself, any more than one forgot how to swim or ride a bicycle. She leant a little forward, and pressed the smooth stock hard into her shoulder. There must be no tell-tale bruise from the recoil.

It was a sitting target if ever there was one, and not more than thirty feet away. Venetia screwed up her eyes and aimed carefully. She firmed her finger on the trigger, and squeezed it, once and a second time. I hadn't forgotten how, she thought; and watched coldly as Mike jerked upright, and staggered, and plunged forward against the handrail of the bridge, and through it, and into the water. The ducks had risen noisily from the lake at the noise, but they settled once more and the ripples dissipated themselves as the body sank. She did not wait to see whether it rose again. She did not want to know whether she had shot to frighten or shot to kill.

Nobody doubted, Hugh Sennen least of all, that he had shot Michael Roper; that Michael Roper had fallen wounded from the bridge, been caught on its broken strut by his trousers, and drowned in the shallow, slimy water of the lake. His body was not found until two days after Hugh had fired the supposedly fatal shot.

The police, doctors, reporters, friends, post mortem and inquest came and went. The episode provided all the drama that a columnist could hope for. Professional man breaking into house, landowner taking violent action against intruder, picturesque estates, decayed beauty spots, historic names and, as a makeweight, a child who found the body. Harriet had illicitly got out of bed at dawn to see whether her pregnant guinea pig had produced her young, and been seduced by the pearly mist of dawn into going for a barefoot walk. She'd rushed back to bed and been found at breakfast time still with the covers clutched over her head, but had been supposed to be suffering from music-lessonitis, rather than any more definite misery. It was not until she collapsed hysterical over the piano keys and was returned to her home still muttering about men, and shoes, and water and weeds that the cause of her distress was revealed. When she had made the horrible discovery she had been too afraid of punishment for getting out of bed in the middle of the night to mention it to her parents.

It was a gem, of course, not just to the newspapers

which unearthed ancient photographs of Hugh as a 'Debs' delight', but to the serious journals which discussed self-protection in a lawless age, the landowner's right to defend his own, the father's need to guard his family from attack. Was it self-defence to shoot an intruder? Was it every Briton's right to take up arms against the enemy's aggression? How far could the doctrine of self-defence be carried?

The magistrates were clearly very reluctant to commit Hugh to be tried for murder. They recalled a case a few years back when magistrates in not unsimilar circumstances had actually refused to do so. But Hugh was remanded in custody. The more hysterical of Venetia's supporters talked to her on the telephone about him as though he were a Tolpuddle martyr or a village Hamden, who had performed not a criminal but a meritorious act. Reporting restrictions had been lifted at the hearing.

Venetia visited Hugh every day in the county gaol. She had been there before when she was going through the magistrate's training course, but then had been the only member of her probationary group who had not said, 'Here, but for the Grace of God, I'd be.' She had never thought of herself as capable of crime in those days. Hugh would hardly discuss the case. He displayed the stoicism which he had reserved in the past for toothache or sunburn, and insisted that the remand wing was neither uncomfortable nor less free than his public school had been. He had done what he had done, and would not whine or make excuses.

Once Lindsay went with Venetia to visit him. The police had been interviewing him repeatedly.

He reminded Venetia of some massive, dignified animal beset by flies. He was baffled at their persistence. 'They seem to think I had some reason for being the feller's

174

enemy,' Hugh said. His hair was a little more grey around the temples, but otherwise events had left no visible mark on him, and he behaved with his usual absent-minded courtesy. 'Why won't they believe I didn't know him from Adam?'

'Perhaps,' Lindsay said softly, 'they thought you took a fraternal interest in your sister-in-law's affairs.'

'What are you talking about?'

'They may have thought you were outraged at the threat to my virtue.'

'What do you mean?' Venetia said. Lindsay glanced at her, with a blank, calm face.

'After all, he was one of my boy friends,' Lindsay said. 'The police up here would have found that out even if I hadn't told them. I don't suppose I was invisible when I went to his place.'

'I didn't know you knew him,' Hugh exclaimed. 'I thought they were making such a meal of it because he was a professional man, not just a layabout. But that must be what they meant. Some of their questions were quite incomprehensible.'

'One of your boy friends?' Venetia said.

'Yes. Didn't you know?'

'You didn't say so, Lindsay,' Hugh said suspiciously.

'I didn't think it would have to be mentioned. It complicates the whole affair, doesn't it? Especially if they think you knew. I'm sorry, Hugh, to bring extra trouble on you. But I suppose he must have broken in because of me. I must have said something about the collections. He couldn't have known I was at Senhouse, I told him days before that I was going back to Africa as soon as possible. Though I shall have to stay to give evidence now.'

'Is that what you told the police?' Venetia asked.

'Yes, I did. And that's what I shall say in court too.'

Lindsay had heard from Colin in Africa. He had quarrelled with the replacement girl and wanted Lindsay to join him as soon as possible. She booked a seat on an aeroplane for the day after Hugh was to come up for trial, and having done so in the travel agency in Halemouth, continued by train to London, whence she telephoned to tell Venetia that she had decided to spend a few days with a friend.

Venetia carried on a life suddenly translated from normality into a cartoon of it; she shopped, they ate, Mrs Best, avid for gossip, made a sketchy pretence of cleaning; Harriet had nightmares, Henry grew aggressive, and Ann Sennen spent a lot of time fruitlessly on the telephone to her influential friends.

Four weeks after the day on which Hugh had been imprisoned first, Lindsay came back, and Venetia, having visited her husband in prison, went on to pick up her sister at the station.

Lindsay was wearing the sort of clothes she had despised on Venetia, and had done her hair in a formal, old-fashioned style. She seemed embarrassed, and did not meet Venetia's eye. Venetia pulled the car into the same wood where once before she had talked in private to her sister on the way from Halemouth to Senhouse.

'It's no use, Venetia, I don't want to talk about it,' Lindsay said, plaiting the chain of her shoulder bag into a knot.

'I didn't want to talk either, at first,' Venetia said. 'I felt so furious with you. And then I realised it couldn't be true, about you and Mike. I wasn't thinking straight. Why did you say it? Was it to protect me?'

'Well, nobody gives a damn about my sex life. It seemed sensible.'

'But they can prove it was me. Lots of people saw me.'

'Look, just don't sit beside me in the court where they can compare our faces, and wear country clothes. You don't want Hugh to feel worse than he must already. It's one thing to kill someone in defence of your family, that won't lie on his conscience. But one's wife's lover is quite another matter.'

'You're right, I suppose. I think he's been protected by feeling in the right, up to now. He's always so certain, you know, doesn't worry about other people's opinions so long as he's made up his mind. What goes on outside the estate isn't quite real to him, I sometimes think. Do you know what I mean?'

'No, but it sounds as though I'm right about not letting him know about your goings on.'

Venetia had expected the children to give trouble the next morning, Harriet because she wanted to share in any drama that was going and Henry because he understood what was going on. The two women and the two children got up early, but there was no trouble, and Venetia was ready to get dressed in good time.

'Wear that awful purple suit with a hat,' Lindsay told her. 'And can I borrow the black dress?' Harriet ran ahead of them to get the dress from Venetia's cupboard. She wrinkled her nose, and handed it to her aunt.

'It smells of your scent already, not Mummy's,' she said. 'I don't like it.'

'That's rude, Harriet,' Venetia told her. When had Lindsay borrowed this dress? It had only come back from the cleaners the day before Venetia wore it on that last trip to London.

They dropped the children at school, and went on to Halemouth. They were trailed from Senhouse by several cars full of reporters and photographers. Ann Sennen had spent the night in the town with a friend.

Venetia found a space to park her car near the court, ignoring the yellow lines. She waited before opening the door. Hugh's solicitor was hastening towards them, trying

177

to push the press representatives aside. 'Lindsay, are you sure?' she said urgently.

'Of course I am. Who cares who I slept with? It won't hurt me.'

The solicitor jerked the door open, and tried to help Venetia out as though she were an old, delicate lady.

'Hugh's in very good spirits,' he said solicitously. 'Don't worry, it will be all right. The prosecution will accept a plea of guilty to the lesser offence. I was a bit afraid—there seemed some doubt, because of someone in your family knowing the deceased.' He shielded his mouth from Lindsay's eyes, and spoke low into Venetia's ear. The photographers, some of whom knew Lindsay as a colleague, were concentrating on her.

Venetia, who was used to courts, had never seen one where the public benches were not only full, but filled by the middle classes. People were bowing and waving and smiling, to her and to each other, as though this were a party of some kind. Lindsay went to sit with Ann Sennen and Venetia joined the solicitor at his table behind the barristers.

Hugh appeared in the dock, coming like a Jack-in-the-box from the cells. The judge came in to respectful bows. He was notorious (to an extent commented on by radical journals, some of which had even suggested that he no longer fulfilled the terms on which he was to hold office—during good behaviour) for his fierce treatment of criminals and unrestrained comments on their counsel. He made no secret that he regretted being unable to give sentences of flogging, and even hanging. He was frequently overturned by the court of appeal.

Hugh was charged not with murder but with manslaughter, and pleaded guilty. Amongst those who understood the procedure, there was a perceptible deflating of tension. The solicitor whispered to Venetia, 'That means there'll be no need to call witnesses to what happened.'

The prosecuting counsel stood up, and related the facts of the case in an almost bored way. He told the court how Michael Roper had been in financial difficulties. He lived above the earnings of himself and his wife, and kept a succession of what the barrister called lady friends. From one of them—a fact admitted by the lady in question, whose photograph, by the way, had been identified by Roper's office staff—he had learnt of the existence of the Senhouse collection. The lady had mentioned to him that the collection was not protected by modern methods of security, and that it had not been catalogued or photographed for insurance purposes.

Several days before the fatal night Michael Roper had been seen in the village of Senhouse. His photograph had been recognised by several people who lived there; he had also, as it happened, been seen in Halemouth in the same week, with his lady friend, who was, in fact, the sister-in-law of the prisoner.

(At this point, nearly everyone in the court room swivelled to look at Lindsay. Venetia pulled her felt hat further over her head. She could see Christine Roper, sitting beside the pimply boy from Mike's office, staring at Lindsay.)

Michael Roper, the barrister continued, had entered Senhouse through an unbolted side door. (He made a joke, worth less than the titter it provoked, about country habits.) Mrs Sennen had woken her husband, who fetched his gun from the room next to the bedroom, and followed the intruder as he went from the house into the grounds. The prisoner had believed, and the prosecution accepted that he believed, that the intruder had turned as though to fire a gun, although no gun had actually been found on his body, or when the lake was dragged. The prisoner fired, and medical evidence showed that Michael Roper had been wounded. The wound would not of itself have killed him. However, the deceased fainted, with his face in the water of the lake. The prisoner, knowing that he could not have done severe damage at the range from which he had fired, and believing that he had frightened the intruder away, returned to the house. The telephone and the power in the house were out of order—it appeared that the telephone wire had been wrenched from the wall, as was common practice for burglars to do—and the police were not summoned since it seemed that nothing was missing. Unfortunately the deceased had died whilst unconscious, from drowning. His clothes had caught on a broken strut of the bridge, and his body was found there by the prisoner's young daughter, not on the next day, but the day after. The body had been identified by the widow.

Hugh having pleaded guilty, and the facts of the case not being in dispute, the court now only needed evidence about the accused, to help decide on a suitable sentence.

The counsel for the defence invited a police officer to give what was called evidence of antecedents: he said there was no previous conviction and the prisoner had behaved in an exemplary manner while in custody.

The Lord-Lieutenant of the County and the Chairman of the County Council were called as witnesses to Hugh's excellent character.

Defence counsel made a plea in mitigation; Hugh's duty to protect his wife and small children, not to mention his property; his isolated house, out of reach of immediate help from the authorities; his outstanding record on National Service in Cyprus, where he had a commission in the Royal Marines—and the instantaneous reactions he had learnt. It was hardly surprising after that training, the barrister commented, that he should, in a split second, have fired before he could be, as he feared, shot. It was a well-known fact that there had been a series of armed robberies in the locality ... increasingly violent society, dangerous times to live in, the duty of every citizen to be vigilant ... other break-ins in the county, sub-post-masters shot in their beds in the next county, whole families murdered by robbers in Yorkshire. The fact that the deceased had acquired some knowledge of the treasures at Senhouse from a lady who was perhaps more misguided than malicious, and that he was not a member of an organised gang of armed thieves, could hardly be known in the heat of the moment. And then he said some more about the respect in which Hugh was held in the district. Somehow by the end of his speech a listener might have been forgiven for supposing Hugh to be a saint and not a sinner.

If they'd investigated possible motives, Venetia thought, we'd be sunk. They would be sure it was a *crime passionel.* Her fingerprints must be all over the office. And if she and Lindsay were side by side in their usual clothes, it would be hard to mistake one for the other. Thank goodness for what the solicitor had told her was the English accusatorial legal system, in which motives and antecedents were irrelevant where the facts were clear.

The judge made a speech before pronouncing the sentence. He talked about living in a lawless age, about the rights of citizens, about property, about protection. Into the middle of this almost exculpatory speech he inserted the warning that people should not take the law into their own hands. But he went on to list circumstances in which it would be forgivable.

181

The solicitor took Venetia's hand and whispered, 'We're home and dry.'

Hugh was put on probation for three years.

They leaned against the gate under the thunder clouds, the air a hot weight on them. Bales were piled at intervals on the harvested fields. The dog made futile dashes at nothing and returned panting to lie at their feet.

'All the same, I did kill a man,' Hugh said. 'You must let me do as I think best.' He had decided to shut half of the house, sell one car and make do with only the old Land Rover, and open the pagoda and shrubbery to the public. Henry's school fees were provided for, and Ann Sennen might help with Harriet's. There would be no more vintage Madeira.

'You don't intend to support the Ropers for the rest of your life?' Venetia protested.

'You don't know what it is to feel this guilt. I must do what Michael Roper would have done.'

'He was going to leave them. His wife meant nothing to him.'

Hugh did not ask how she knew. He had cut Lindsay, the supposed instigator of his troubles, out of his consciousness. He intended neither to resent her nor to think of her at all. She had gone to join Colin in Africa, and did not expect to be back, she told Venetia, until Hugh had had time to forgive her. But it didn't make much difference to her if he never did. She felt that the only way he had changed was in focusing his disapproval.

'It needn't make all that much difference to your life,' Hugh said. 'I'll try not to let it. None of this is your fault.'

What had Lindsay meant when she said that Venetia

183

should be truthful with Hugh, and urged her to see that they talked? She was wrong, Venetia thought, to be so sure of the value of clarification and discussions. It would not relieve Hugh of his burden of guilt to know that his wife's was no less. For Hugh was less innocent than Lindsay and the world supposed.

He must know as well as Venetia did—though it was like most important things in their lives, left unsaid—that the defence he had accepted and profited by was not true. He had never supposed Mike Roper to be carrying a gun. He'd recognised the act of throwing and felt the fall of the missile; indeed, before Mike turned to throw his loot at his pursuer, it was clear that he was set on escape, not attack. Hugh had simply reverted to the type of his ancestor who set man-traps for poachers; he'd acted with deliberation, furious certainly, but not seeing red, not on the spur of the moment, not shooting in a split second before being shot. Venetia had half-expected him to refuse to accept the miscarriage of justice, and to deny the half-truth in open court.

Ann Sennen did not know that her son's guilt was greater than the one he admitted to. But she understood his mind better than Venetia did. She'd said that so long as he was in prison on remand he was the conforming, obedient citizen he had learnt to portray at school and Cambridge and in the army. He acted the part expected of him so thoroughly that he believed in it. Once back at Senhouse he became a different person, insulated from public opinion by the fences that surrounded his acres. Here he would justify his actions by the standards of the paterfamilias. If he could live with himself he would not care if the rest of the world refused to live with him.

But then Ann Sennen did not know what had really happened either. Presumably she too believed the story of apparent self-defence. She would be proud of Hugh's concern for the Ropers. Venetia knew he would be paying conscience money.

Lindsay had said he had a right to know on whose conscience the burden should really fall. They'd been on the way to the station, Venetia seeing her off on the first lap of the long journey away from Senhouse, and perhaps away from her sister's life. Lindsay said a lot, after a long silence, assuming to herself the didactic, admonitory elder-sister's role, showing herself to be observant where Venetia had thought her blind, wise where she had seemed unconcerned.

'You need some truth between yourself and Hugh,' Lindsay said. 'More than you've had, at any rate.'

'About Mike, do you think?'

'As far as the affair went, perhaps. I'm not sure about the rest. He'll have it on his conscience, won't he?'

'Can you wonder?' Venetia said.

'Is it fair, when it should be on yours?' Venetia gaped, and Lindsay went on, 'The body wasn't there in the morning after Mike broke in. I went down to the lake, before breakfast. I was helping Hugh look for anything the burglar might have dropped. He didn't come further than the lawn, but I thought I'd check.'

'You didn't say anything—'

'I decided to wait and see. And then it seemed best to keep quiet about it, not having been there then, when I found it later in the day. It was pouring, do you remember, and you'd gone to fetch the children. The dog was whining down by the lake and I went to see what was wrong.'

Venetia still gaped at her, with her hand clamped over her mouth. Lindsay went on, 'So I guessed. Oh, perhaps not exactly what happened, I'm not sure that I know that even now. But I knew it was Mike Roper. I'd met him in Halemouth. I could imagine what complications there would be. I didn't know he'd been shot, but it was bad

185

enough having him there at all, from your point of view. But there seemed no reason why Hugh shouldn't think it was me that was Mike's girl friend, and anyone else who had seen you with him. It never seemed an advantage to be so alike before.'

'What did you do?'

'Actually I put on one of your Londony dresses and a headscarf and went to his office. He'd given me the address, and said something that implied you'd met him there. It was dead easy to get in, the lock was no better than an ordinary door handle. I learnt how to do much more difficult ones than that in my drop-out phase. I was surprised at you, the squalor! Anyway, I scattered some fingerprints around, just in case, and checked that he didn't have a signed photograph of you or anything. It just seemed a sensible precaution, that's all, though the police never took my prints in the end.'

'But Lindsay, why? I mean, if you believe in having the truth with everything, in not acting—?'

'In my personal life, not when it's the state or the law. Colin thinks it's the positive duty of the free citizen to foil the power of the state. Actually, I don't know that it was worth the effort. Do you think anyone checked? It must have seemed so obviously true—I mean, that he was my boy friend. I don't suppose it would have crossed anyone's mind that you had ever so much as set foot in that part of London, let alone touched a man like Mike Roper.'

Venetia did not know how to accept Lindsay's care for her. She had never before been the one to receive, part of her envy of Lindsay's free and untrammelled life had rested on the fact that Lindsay gave cause for concern but never had occasion to feel it for anyone else.

'But Hugh has the right to know,' Lindsay said. The car was going through the town's suburbs, and Venetia pulled her dark glasses from the shelf to hide her from curious eyes. She'd once liked the feeling of being known by more people in the town than she knew.

The station forecourt was crowded. Venetia wondered whether Halemouth and Senhouse would now be the boundaries of her life. She scented a whiff of freedom and anonymity; and it was gone.

Lindsay gathered up her bags and swung her legs out of the car.

'After the way you said you disapproved of my life,' Venetia asked her, 'why did you do it?'

'I felt sorry for you. This life is all you've got.' Lindsay leant back into the car and kissed Venetia's cheek. Several people were watching them with a new, blatant interest. 'Don't get out, the sixth Mrs Sennen, or do I mean the seventh? Anyway, goodbye.' She walked jauntily into the station. What if Christine Roper was on the train? Lindsay wouldn't know her by sight. Oh, it was all too complicated. Anyway, that dignified woman would hardly speak to Lindsay in the circumstances. Venetia thought, I give up. She drove straight back to Senhouse.

She thought of that unexpected conversation now, as she and Hugh stood together at the gate of the barley field.

What were Mr and Mrs Andrews discussing as Gainsborough painted their secure figures beside their stooks of corn? Had they withdrawn suspicious eyes from anguished reappraisal of their lives for long enough to let the painter portray their security? Was their assured appearance a façade? Perhaps Mrs Andrews was riven by the urge to confess and the determination not to. Venetia pressed her lips together. In their own way she and Hugh would represent their own class and century to the future. It would only add to Hugh's burden to feel guilty on her behalf. For in this too he would see a unity between husband and wife. But only in one direction, it seemed: he did not regard Venetia as tarred by the brush which had blackened him.

187

'It won't change your life much,' he said again.

'My life, or the seventh Mrs Sennen's?'

'What do you mean?'

'Perhaps it really is the same thing.'

'I don't know what you're talking about. I don't like it when you go in for this introspective talk. You get it from your sister.'

'Don't you see any difference between me, the real me, and the public lady who opens fêtes and sits on the bench? There must be a person behind the label, propping up the façade, mustn't there? Or perhaps the medium really is the message.'

'Are you feeling all right, darling? I'm afraid all this has been too much for you.'

'But as you once said, it doesn't really matter. So long as the job gets done, who cares if behind the image there's nobody there. And I'm the one who went to all lengths to preserve the image. You can add my portrait to the row in the dining-room: the seventh Mrs Sennen, conformist. No one will know the difference, when I'm an ancestor, too.'

Hugh had taken Venetia's arm and turned back towards the house. They walked along the lane, and then into the garden, and across the terrace. He stood picking pieces of lichen off a stone urn. 'What are you trying to tell me?' he asked.

'Nothing, nothing at all.'

'I expect you're overwrought,' he said kindly. 'You'll be all right in the morning. What have you got on tomorrow?'

They went into the house, and Venetia opened the engagement diary. The telephone rang, and she answered it and handed the receiver to him. 'It's Colonel Wilton.'

Hugh listened for a long time, saying, 'Yes,' and 'I see,' at intervals. When he rang off he said, 'I don't know how to tell you. I feel so very much to blame.'

'What is it?'

'He didn't have the heart to tell you himself. Wilton, of all people—! The very last ... anyway. The thing is this. They seem to think it might be awkward—embarrassing— if you appear on the bench. Not that you have done anything, of course, there's no suggestion of that. I think it's nonsense. You could brazen it out.'

'Do they want me to resign?'

'Well, from what he said, I don't quite ... yes. Actually, darling, I think, yes. They do. I cannot express to you how mortified I am. Forgive me.'

The diary had fallen open at the next week's page. Venetia picked up a pencil, and made a careful line through the words 'Motoring Court' on Monday, and 'Juvenile Court' on Thursday. Then she crossed out Red Cross Committee, and all the other public engagements, more and more quickly, turning the pages and slashing through the neat writing. She had a feeling of liberation, of shedding a load. She threw the mutilated little book into a drawer, and gazed at her reflection in the glass. She said, 'Who is left when the seventh Mrs Sennen is gone?'